THE MYSTERY OF THE
Dead Man's Riddle

The Three Investigators heard a thump—like a heavy board hitting the ground. They rushed to the railing of the houseboat and saw a dark figure on shore running into the trees.

"The houseboat's loose!" cried Bob.

Their gangplank lay on the ground along with the mooring lines. The boat was ten feet from shore and drifting downstream fast.

"Look!" Pete shouted. "The dam!"

Straight ahead of them, the swollen stream poured over a rocky dam in a mass of roaring water!

The Three Investigators in

THE MYSTERY OF THE
Dead Man's
Riddle

By William Arden

Based on characters created by Robert Arthur

Random House 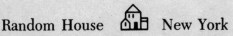 New York

Originally published by Random House in 1974.
Revised edition, 1984.

Library of Congress Cataloging in Publication Data:
Arden, William 1924–. The Three Investigators in
   The mystery of the dead man's riddle.
   (The Three Investigators mystery series ; 22)
   Originally published under title: Alfred Hitchcock and The Three
Investigators in The mystery of the dead man's riddle.
   SUMMARY: Three young detectives go on a high-stakes treasure hunt in
order to restore a fortune to the rightful heirs.
   [1. Mystery and detective stories]   I. Arthur, Robert.
II. Title.   III. Title: Mystery of the dead man's riddle.
IV. Series. PZ7.A6794Td 1984   [Fic]   83-23083
ISBN: 0-394-86422-0 (pbk.)

Manufactured in the United States of America
   3   4   5   6   7   8   9   0

Contents

	An Introduction by Hector Sebastian	*vii*
1.	Dingo Towne's Challenge	*3*
2.	Where the Wild Dog Lives	*9*
3.	New Enemies—And Old!	*17*
4.	Jupiter Finds the Key	*25*
5.	The Bottle and Stopper	*30*
6.	A Dangerous Prank	*37*
7.	Pete Takes Over	*42*
8.	Unexpected Visitors	*50*
9.	A Ride from a Friend	*57*
10.	A Reckless Driver	*65*
11.	The Tenth Ball of Twine	*70*
12.	The Old Bushranger	*75*

13. Danger Ahead!   81

14. Pete Finds the Handsome Mug   88

15. Get Out If You Can!   94

16. Another Riddle Solved   100

17. Caught!   104

18. A Near Miss   112

19. Dead Man's Laugh!   117

20. Jupiter Sets a Trap   125

21. Pete Saves the Day   133

22. Jupiter Confesses an Error!   140

An Introduction
by Hector Sebastian

Hi, mystery lovers.

You're about to delve into the mysterious riddles of an old friend of mine—Marcus "Dingo" Towne. Dingo was as eccentric in death as he was in life. Get set to read his last will and testament—and not understand a word of it! At least, that was my reaction—and I'm one of the executors. To solve the riddles, the family called in a crack junior detective team, The Three Investigators.

If you've never had the pleasure of being introduced to my young friends, let me do the honors. Meet Jupiter Jones, the stout First Investigator and deductive genius of the three. Next is Pete Crenshaw, the athletic Second Investigator. And last but by no means least is Bob Andrews, the studious boy who's in charge of Records and Research. All three live near Hollywood in the town of Rocky Beach, California, where Dingo challenged all comers to solve his riddles.

From Jupiter's first brainstorm into the key behind the dead man's message, the team ran up against greedy schemers and hidden menaces. And in the end they learned that the solution of a riddle isn't always the last word!

But that's enough for now. You'll soon find out that

everything is not what it seems when an unconventional man speaks after he is dead! Read on at your own risk—this time even Jupiter failed to see one clue that was right in front of him.

Who knows, maybe *you'll* catch what Jupiter missed if you have the nerve to unravel the dead man's riddle!

—HECTOR SEBASTIAN

THE MYSTERY OF THE
Dead Man's Riddle

1 ✦ Dingo Towne's Challenge

It was an hour before dinner on a spring Wednesday in Rocky Beach, California. Bob Andrews, the Records and Research man of The Three Investigators, was in his room writing up the trio's latest case—a minor affair of finding Mrs. Hester's lost diamond ring. From outside came the sounds of neighborhood children playing in the late afternoon sunshine. A car door banged close by; Bob's father had arrived home from work.

A few moments later Mr. Andrews came into Bob's room, grinning. He carried a long piece of paper.

"How would you and your detective friends like to find a fortune," Mr. Andrews said, "and keep it all!"

"Gosh, Dad," the blond boy said, "you mean someone lost a fortune, and if we find it we can keep it?"

"It isn't lost," Mr. Andrews said. "It's hidden!"

"Gee, it can't be much of a fortune if someone's giving it away. Unless he's crazy, maybe."

"I don't know what kind of fortune it is, but I think crazy is the right word, all right." Mr. Andrews laughed, then rubbed his chin. "Still, I see your Mr. Sebastian is involved, so maybe it's not so crazy. Here, Bob, you can read it."

Mr. Andrews held out the long sheet of paper. It was a galley proof from the newspaper on which Mr. Andrews worked.

"We're printing the story tomorrow," he explained to Bob, "but I thought you boys might like an advance look, eh?"

Bob took the galley and read:

WEALTHY ECCENTRIC LEAVES CHALLENGE: FIND HIS FORTUNE—AND KEEP IT!

"Crazy" Will Is Proof of Mental Illness Declares Family Lawyer

The late recluse and mystery man, Marcus ("Dingo") Towne, who died last Sunday in Rocky Beach, has apparently left his entire fortune to anyone who can find it!

The unexpected development came yesterday when Mr. Towne's long-time friend John ("Jack") Dillon filed a surprise will for probate. Mr. Towne, a mysterious eccentric in Rocky Beach for twenty years, always wore shabby clothes and lived in a ramshackle old house, but was widely thought to be a millionaire.

Mr. Roger Callow, representing Mr. Towne for the Rocky Beach law firm of Sink and Waters, declared the secret will to be proof that Mr. Towne was no longer in his right mind. "We know a legitimate will exists that leaves everything to his daughter-in-law and grandson," Mr. Callow stated.

The surprise will, written in longhand, was witnessed by Mr. Dillon and another friend, Mrs. Sadie Jingle.

The article then printed the entire will, which Bob read with growing excitement.

"Wow, can I show this to Pete and Jupe, Dad? There's time before dinner!"

Mr. Andrews laughed and nodded. Bob dashed to the

phone to call his friends, then hurried to his bike. He pedaled rapidly to The Jones Salvage Yard, a fabulous junkyard owned by Jupiter Jones's aunt and uncle. Not wishing to run into Aunt Mathilda Jones, a formidable woman who always wanted to put the boys to work, Bob proceeded past the junkyard's main gate and stopped at the far corner. Here was Green Gate One, one of The Three Investigators' private entrances to the yard. Bob pushed up two loose, green-painted boards and stepped directly into Jupe's outdoor workshop.

When he found no one there, Bob dropped his bike and pushed aside an iron grating that seemed to lean casually against Jupiter's workbench. Behind it was the mouth of a large, galvanized pipe. This was Tunnel Two, which led under piles of junk to the secret headquarters of The Three Investigators. Headquarters was a damaged old house trailer which Uncle Titus Jones had given to Jupiter when he found he couldn't sell it. Except for the tools in Jupiter's workshop, Headquarters was equipped with everything The Investigators needed for their work: an office desk, telephone, tape recorder, darkroom, miniature laboratory, and assorted pieces of detective equipment, mostly rebuilt from junk. Outside, the boys had piled so much junk around the trailer that no one could see it anymore, and by now everyone else had forgotten it was there.

Bob crawled through Tunnel Two, which ended underneath Headquarters, and entered the trailer through a trap door. Jupiter and Pete were waiting.

"What's this about a will, Records?" Jupiter Jones asked. The stocky First Investigator looked like a round-faced young owl, especially when he was thinking—which was most of the time. He was the "brains" of the trio, and liked to prove it!

"Will, shmill," Pete Crenshaw said. "What about the fortune?"

The Second Investigator was taller and stronger than his buddies—big, athletic, and the most happy-go-lucky of the trio. He leaned forward eagerly as Bob handed the galley to Jupiter, who read the will aloud:

I, Marcus Towne, being of a lot sounder mind than most men, especially my relatives and their friends, and one who made his pile by hard work and quick brains, see no reason to leave it all to shiftless, greedy, stupid, and otherwise useless people who liked my money more than they liked me!

Therefore, in this my last will and testament, I bequeath to my daughter-in-law, my grandson, my niece, and my nephew the sum of $1.00 each! The remainder of my estate I give, without reservations, to anyone who can find my treasure!

As an aid for the more intelligent, if there are any, I leave this set of riddles. Solve them and find the loot!

Where the wild dog lives, the bottle and stopper
show the way to the billabong.

Above the apples and pears all alone
the Lady from Bristol rides from a friend.

At the tenth ball of twine, you and me
see our handsome mug ahead.

One man's victim is another's darlin',
follow the nose to the place.

Where men buy their trouble and strife,
get out if you can.

> *In the posh Queen's old Ned, be bright
> and natural and the prize is yours!*

Who'd have thought the old man had so much money in him? Roll the dice and the swag is yours!

Executors will be: John Dillon, who likes me; Sink and Waters, who like money; Hector Sebastian, who likes mystery!

Jupiter, who had once been a child actor on TV, finished dramatically and beamed at the others.

"Wow," Pete said at last. "A dead man's riddle! Is that a real will, Jupe? Or just a crazy joke?"

"Oh, I assume it's real," said Jupe. "I mean, if you solve the riddles, I assume you *will* find Mr. Towne's fortune. But I don't know if the will is legal—if the person who found the treasure would be allowed to keep it. But even if the will *is* legal, I imagine the family will go to court and claim that the old man was crazy and his will is invalid. Still"—and his eyes sparkled— "I wonder what he hid, and where."

The one thing Jupiter could never resist was a challenge to his brain, a puzzle of any kind.

"Maybe Mr. Sebastian knows if it's legal," Bob said.

"An excellent thought," Jupiter agreed. He reached for the telephone and dialed Mr. Sebastian's number. Mr. Sebastian was a detective turned mystery writer. He had become the boys' mentor and found cases for them from time to time. When Mr. Sebastian answered, Jupiter explained why he was calling.

"Jupe, you beat me to it." The mystery writer's voice came out of the loudspeaker Jupiter had rigged up so that they all could listen to a phone conversation at once. "I was just about to call you. Dingo has outdone himself. The whole town is buzzing with his cockamamie will—and no one can make head or tail of it."

"I agree that it is baffling," Jupiter said, "but is it legal? If someone were to find what he hid, would they be entitled to keep it?"

"Oh, for the time being it's quite legal—nutty, but legal. Look, Jupe, I'll put it to you straight. This will may be declared invalid in court, but that may take a long time. Meanwhile there may be a case here for The Three Investigators. The family called me to let me know they're concerned. So I suggested your firm."

"Thank you, Mr. Sebastian," said Jupiter. "We'd be honored to help. But what exactly are they worried about?"

"Sorry, I've got a call on my other line," said Mr. Sebastian. "Straighten it out with the Townes if they call. Gotta run." And with that the mystery writer hung up.

"Neat," said Pete sarcastically. "We're supposed to decipher a will that's bound to be thrown out of court."

"Don't you see?" said Jupe excitedly. "Even if the court eventually says the treasure belongs to the family, no one knows where the treasure is! The riddles still have to be solved. And that's where we come in."

The other two Investigators brightened. They might be instrumental in finding a fortune for Dingo's rightful heirs. The three boys agreed to meet at Headquarters the next day before school. Jupiter would spend the evening in Headquarters near the phone.

2 ✦ Where the Wild Dog Lives

Early next morning, Pete ate a hurried breakfast and rode his bike to the salvage yard. Jupiter hadn't called to report anything from the Townes. As the Second Investigator neared Green Gate One, he saw Bob crouched at the fence.

"Did Jupe call you?" Pete exclaimed.

"No," Bob whispered, "and someone's sneaking around HQ!"

Pete crouched beside his smaller chum and peered in through the secret opening in the front fence. Beyond the workshop area, he saw someone moving among the mounds of junk that hid the trailer. Neither boy could see the intruder clearly in the long morning shadows, but whoever it was seemed to be pulling aside junk to look in!

"Is Jupe inside?" Pete whispered. "We'd better warn him—"

"Look!"

Bob pointed to the opening of Tunnel Two under Jupe's workbench. Jupiter's pale round face loomed behind the cover grating.

"He's heard the guy," Bob whispered.

Jupe caught the whisper, put his finger to his lips, and rolled his eyes upward. Then he motioned toward the rear of the junkyard.

"He wants us to circle around," Bob said softly. "Chase whoever it is into the workshop where we can grab him!"

The two boys ran softly around to the rear of the yard where there was another secret opening in the fence. Slipping inside, they crept forward past piles of junk. They stopped close to Headquarters, crouched behind a stack of old washing machines, and peeked out. The shadowy figure was still there, trying to find a way through the junk surrounding the trailer. Pete jumped up.

"Stand right where you are!" the tall boy yelled.

The figure whirled, slipped on some loose junk, and fell. He scrambled up—a very small boy!

"Grab him!" Bob cried.

The Investigators charged. With a frightened cry, the small boy turned and ran—right toward the workshop. He cast a glance back at Pete and Bob and never saw Jupiter come out of the pipe ahead. Jupiter ran forward and grabbed him. The little boy struggled wildly.

"Let me go! Let me go!"

He was no more than eight, thin and wiry, with wild black hair and big, dark eyes. He wore blue jeans, a black sweatshirt, and black sneakers.

"Why are you spying on us?" Jupiter demanded.

The boy suddenly stopped struggling. Pete and Bob ran up. The little boy looked at them wide-eyed.

"You're The Three Investigators, aren't you! Gee, you scared me, jumping out like that."

"Why were you searching the junk piles?" Jupiter scowled.

"I know you have an office hidden somewhere in the yard," the small boy said, and grinned proudly. "I know all about you. I live in Rocky Beach, and I'm a detective, too." Then he looked down and scuffed his toe in the dirt. "I mean, I want to be a detective, too. I'm practicing."

"You mean you were looking for us?" Bob said.

The boy nodded eagerly. "I want to hire you. I mean, my mother does anyway, so I came—"

A woman's voice called angrily from across the yard:

"Billy Towne! You march home at once, young man! I told you not to come here!"

A young woman in a bright blue dress appeared among the piles of junk. She had long black hair, flashing brown eyes, and a worried look. She hurried toward the Investigators and the little boy. A tanned young man walked behind her. His brown hair was long, but he wore a conservative blue suit—and a frown.

"Towne?" Jupiter's eyes lit up. "Mr. and Mrs. Towne?"

"I'm Nelly Towne," the woman said. "My husband is dead. This is Mr. Roger Callow, my fiancé and our lawyer. I'm afraid Billy must come home now. He hasn't even had his breakfast."

Pete was dismayed. "You didn't come to hire us?"

"We sure did!" Billy cried. "To find Granddad's fortune!"

Roger Callow laughed. "Whoa now, Billy. We're not sure we want to hire anyone, even if Mr. Sebastian recommends them. This will is a joke, boys," he explained. "We'll break it in court. Dingo's estate will go to Billy, under California law—unless, of course, we find the real will that leaves the estate to Nelly and Billy."

"Find?" Jupiter said. "Don't you have the older will in your office, sir?"

"We did have it," Roger Callow admitted. "It's missing. We'll probably find it in old Dingo's house somewhere."

"But we haven't found it!" Billy said. "And we don't know where the treasure is! And you even said someone could find it first and steal it all!"

"That's true, Roger," added Mrs. Towne. "It could be stolen easily and we'd never get it back."

Jupiter asked, "Why *easily* stolen?"

Mrs. Towne and Roger Callow looked at each other. The lawyer sighed.

"Old Dingo was an odd man," he said. "He had a nice cottage, but he let Nelly and Billy use that and lived himself in a run-down old house on the same property. He dressed poorly and never spent any money, but we knew he had a fortune. He wouldn't invest it—kept it in banks and in cash. Or so we thought. When he died on Sunday, we searched the old house and found nothing! Not even a bankbook. Then yesterday we learned he'd turned everything into gem-stones. A million dollars' worth of opals, sapphires, rubies, and emeralds!"

"Because," Jupiter realized, "gems take up very little space for their value. They're easy to hide—and easy to steal!"

Roger Callow nodded grimly. "If we don't find those jewels first, we may never see them! Especially if the Percivals get their hands on them. Much they'd care that the fortune belongs to Nelly and Billy!"

"Who are the Percivals, sir?" Bob asked.

"Old Dingo's niece and nephew from London. They're the children of his sister, who died years ago. Dingo never liked them and hadn't seen them in years, but they arrived in Rocky Beach two days after he died. They want the treasure badly."

Jupiter pondered. "Why would Dingo write such a strange will, Mrs. Towne?"

"Because he was old and crazy!" Roger Callow snapped.

"Because," Mrs. Towne answered sadly, "he didn't really like any of his relatives, including Billy and me, and I guess he thought he'd play a good joke on us."

"Some joke!" exclaimed Pete.

"Leaving a will in riddle form *is* a joke," said Jupiter, "but I'm sure the riddles do lead to the jewels. Do you agree?"

"I don't know," answered the lawyer. "But we have nothing else to go on. We know the jewels aren't in Dingo's house, and it would be just like old Dingo to hide his treasure."

"Then why not let us find it for you?" offered Jupe. "We're experienced detectives and—"

"I'm sorry boys," interrupted Mrs. Towne. "Perhaps a real detective agency would—"

"They *are* real detectives, Mom," Billy cried. "Show your card, Jupiter!"

Jupiter whipped the Investigators' business card out of his pocket and gave it to Mrs. Towne. It said:

THE THREE INVESTIGATORS
"We Investigate Anything"
? ? ?

First Investigator .... Jupiter Jones
Second Investigator .... Peter Crenshaw
Records and Research .... Bob Andrews

"Um, that's very nice, boys, but—"

"Jupe, show her the card from Chief Reynolds," urged Pete.

Jupiter produced another card. This one read:

> *This certifies that the bearer is a Volunteer Junior Assistant Deputy cooperating with the police force of Rocky Beach. Any assistance given him will be appreciated.*
>
> *(Signed) Samuel Reynolds*
> *Chief of Police*

Mrs. Towne smiled. "I apologize, boys. You are detectives."

"And perhaps just who we need," Roger Callow said. "From what Billy tells us, you boys have solved some very strange and difficult cases. I wouldn't be surprised if you could solve those riddles faster than any adult. I admit they have me stumped! Nelly? What do you say? Shall we hire The Three Investigators?"

"All right," Mrs. Towne answered.

"Hooray!" yelled Billy. "And I can help, too, can't I, Mom?"

"Certainly not! You're only seven years old, Billy Towne! That's too young to be chasing around the countryside."

"Aw, Mom," muttered the boy. "I'm almost eight."

"You can start at once, boys," said Roger Callow. "Speed is vital—and secrecy."

"Gee," Pete said glumly. "We have to go to school."

"And I don't think there will be total secrecy," added Bob. "I mean, Dingo's will is going to be in the paper today!"

"Oh, no!" groaned Mr. Callow. "We'll have every fortune hunter in the state searching for the treasure! You must hurry, boys!"

"Speed," said Jupiter Jones, "is relative." Jupe had a trick of seeming older and wiser than his years, and now his authoritative tone calmed the lawyer. "The riddles require careful thought. No one is going to solve them by rushing into things. I've studied the will, and I'm sure each riddle must be solved step by step. I'll examine them all again during school, and we'll meet this afternoon where the first riddle says to begin."

"And where would that be, young man?" Roger Callow asked.

"Why," Jupiter said triumphantly, "where the wild dog lives, of course." He took a copy of the will from his pocket and read:

> *"Where the wild dog lives, the bottle and stopper show the way to the billabong."*

He grinned. "A dingo is an Australian wild dog," he said, drawing on his encyclopedic knowledge. "And a billabong is a stream or water hole in Australia. So, we meet at Dingo's house, and look for a bottle with a stopper that points toward some water!"

3 ⟐ New Enemies—And Old!

The moment school ended that day, the boys headed for Dingo Towne's house. It was just inside the city limits of Rocky Beach, next to the Botanical Gardens and a large county park. As the boys rode their bikes up a hill a block from Dingo's house, Jupiter said:

"We must remember to be discreet, fellows. On a sensitive case like this one, we don't want to draw any attention to ourselves."

"Att–attention, Jupe?" Pete stammered. "Look!"

They had reached the top of the hill. Below and to their left lay Dingo's spacious property, surrounded by a tumble-down fence and littered with junk, old lumber, and mounds of bottles. To one side was a neat white cottage. In the center stood a dilapidated old house with sagging walls. But the boys weren't staring at the house!

There was a mob scene below! People were everywhere, swarming over the property like ants! From small boys to old women, they ran madly about, trampling bushes, digging holes, pulling at the piles of bottles and trash. Pandemonium filled the spring afternoon as fights broke out and people screamed at each other.

"It's mine!" . . . "I found it!" . . . "Let go the bottle!"

The boys could see Chief Reynolds and his men

trying to control the horde. They rode down through the melee and up to the cottage, where Mrs. Towne, Billy, and Roger Callow watched in dismay.

"They'll ruin the clues," Billy wailed.

"Broken bottles everywhere," Jupiter observed calmly. "Why are there so many?"

"Because Dingo collected bottles," Roger Callow fumed. "Hundreds of them! Thousands! Now we'll never find the right one!"

Chief Reynolds came up mopping his brow. A fat man and a skinny woman were behind him. They spoke with English accents.

"Make them all leave, Officer!" the skinny woman demanded.

"Trespassers!" the fat man raged. "Arrest them all!"

Chief Reynolds shook his head wearily. "Your uncle's will gave them permission to come here, Mr. Percival. It would take the Army to disperse this mob. All we can do is protect the houses."

"Our uncle was crazy," the woman said. "We're the owners."

"Oh, no, you're not, Winifred Percival," Mrs. Towne said.

Winifred Percival reddened. "You're not even his flesh and blood, Nelly Towne. This is some scheme to cheat us! I knew we should have come from England sooner and cared for dear Marcus."

"He wouldn't even have you in his house!" Mr. Percival said. "Made you live over here in the cottage!"

Roger Callow said, "He hadn't spoken to you in ten years, Cecil! He wouldn't have let *you* in the house, either! Now, the court will decide who owns what. But the cottage is Mrs. Towne's. Marcus—Dingo—gave it to her years ago, and *you're* trespassing."

"Then she stole the cottage!" Cecil Percival cried.

"The way she's trying to steal his fortune! You and she, Mr. Lawyer Callow!" Winifred Percival raged. "But we know there has to be a real will that names *us* to inherit."

"The real will names Billy and Nelly," Roger Callow said.

Cecil Percival sneered. "So you say, but you conveniently lost that will, eh? You probably forged this crazy one, but we'll break it."

"Then Billy will get everything anyway." Callow smiled. "He's the only direct descendant."

"We're relatives too!" cried Winifred. "We're entitled to a share!"

"Not under California law," replied Callow. "You have no claim to your uncle's fortune if there is a direct descendant."

Both Percivals glared at the little boy, who glared back.

"We'll see about that," Cecil said nastily.

"Please leave my house at once," Mrs. Towne said, looking pale.

The two Percivals turned red as beets.

"We'll get our fortune, you hear?" Winifred said. "We know what belongs to us!"

The two of them stalked away. Chief Reynolds shrugged and moved off to break up a nearby fight among the searchers.

"Wow," Pete said, "those Percivals sure sound mean."

"They are," Roger Callow said. "Disagreeable snobs who thought they were too good to associate with old Dingo—until now! They'll get nothing. Perhaps we'd better start looking for the bottle and stopper clue ourselves. You boys—"

Jupiter broke in, "I think we should go inside, sir."

Without waiting for an answer, the stocky leader of The Three Investigators walked into the cottage. The others followed. Jupiter glanced around the neat living room with its windows open to catch the breeze.

"Did you search the two houses for any bottle that could be a clue to some sort of water?" he asked.

"We sure did," Billy cried, "but we didn't find one."

"No," Jupiter said, "because I don't think there is one!"

He took out his copy of the riddles. "Dingo wants us to start here, somewhere on his property, but he doesn't say so expressly. He says *where the wild dog lives.* That's like poetry—the words don't name something, they sort of describe it, hint at it. A special kind of code!"

"You mean," Bob said slowly, "*bottle and stopper* doesn't mean a real bottle, but maybe something that looks like one?"

"Exactly!" Jupiter said. "Something that looks like a bottle, and points to a place with water."

"I don't think there's anything here that simply looks like a bottle," said Nelly Towne.

"But there's water!" cried Billy. "The duck pond next door in the Botanical Gardens!"

"And look," said Bob, "the next clue is *above the apples and pears all alone.* Isn't there an orchard around that pond?"

Roger Callow was excited. "I think you've hit on it!"

"Well—" Jupiter began.

A snicker suddenly filled the room—a snicker from outside the window! A voice said, "Thanks for the help, dumbheads!" Pete leaped to the window as feet ran away.

"Skinny Norris!" he exclaimed.

A tall, skinny youth was running off toward the Botanical Gardens. E. Skinner Norris himself—a mean, spoiled kid who constantly got in the Investigators' way. Though not much older than the trio, he already had his driver's license because his family lived half the year in another state where the driving age was lower. He also had his own car, a flashy red sports car. He couldn't stand anyone being smarter than he was— which meant he hated the Investigators, especially Jupiter!

"He heard," Pete moaned. "We should've figured Skinny—"

"Never mind," Jupiter interrupted. "He won't get far. The *billabong* clue might mean the duck pond, but *apples and pears* shouldn't mean trees. Too easy. No, it must have some other meaning, fellows. Suggest something else."

Jupiter looked at everyone, but no one spoke. He frowned.

"Perhaps if we knew more about old Dingo," he said, "we'd know how to interpret his riddles."

"Well," Roger Callow said, "he was born in Australia about 1895. His father had been a convict—England sent its convicts to Australia back then. Dingo was a wild boy, became a bushranger—that's a bandit—then made a fortune in opals, but had to run from the law. He went to Canada, made more money, married late, had one son. He came here twenty years ago and lived like a hermit. When his son died five years ago in a car crash, Nelly had nowhere to go, so Dingo let her move in here with Billy. But he wasn't very gracious about it. Old Dingo was suspicious of everyone and wouldn't let anyone in his house. He hated almost everything except Australia, and maybe Cockneys like his father. A rough-and-ready man, boys."

Bob said, "Dingo used the Australian word *billabong* in his riddle, and his nickname is Australian for wild dog. Could *apples and pears* be something Australian or maybe Canadian, sir?"

"Not that I know of, Bob," Callow said. When Mrs. Towne shook her head too, the lawyer sighed. "Perhaps you boys had better go home and think some more. It's getting late."

Billy looked crushed—his heroes had failed. The boys were unhappy, too. As they biked away, they saw that most of the mob was also leaving in defeat. They rode in silence until they had almost reached the salvage yard. Then Pete finally spoke:

"Jupe, what are Cockneys? Mr. Callow said Dingo's dad was a Cockney, and Dingo liked them. Some special Englishmen?"

"From the East End of London," Jupiter answered

without much interest. "Supposedly, anyone born within sound of the Bow bells—the bells of Saint Mary-le-Bow Church. Cockneys have a funny accent —they say *'ot* instead of *hot, blime* instead of *blame.* Australians do it, too."

"They do?" Bob said. "Jupe, maybe the way Australians talk has something to do with the riddles. Maybe in Australia the clues *sound* different. Maybe what they sound like—"

Jupiter sat up so suddenly on his bike that it jerked and almost ran into the salvage yard fence.

"Cockneys!" he exclaimed. "Maybe—!"

Just then Pete saw a familiar car parked across the street from the salvage yard, near the Jones house.

"Jupe! It's Skinny again!"

The red sports car seemed empty, but as they watched, a head moved inside. Skinny Norris never could be patient. He was tailing them!

"Quick," Jupiter said, taking the riddle paper from his pocket. "Pretend we've just discovered something and I'm sending you off to investigate. Ride fast and lead him away. I've got a hunch, and I don't want Skinny to see where I go!"

Skinny took the bait greedily. Bob and Pete heard his car start as they pedaled hard down the block and vanished around a corner. Skinny waited just long enough to see Jupiter casually ride up to his front door, then took off after Pete and Bob.

The two boys led Skinny a merry chase through the streets, pretending they were in a hurry and didn't know he was following. Then they simply rode home!

When Bob turned into his yard, Skinny looked startled. He continued to follow Pete, only to see him turn into his own driveway. Pete looked back and laughed aloud when he saw the anger on Skinny's face. The older boy realized he had been hoodwinked and roared off in a violent cloud of dust.

After dinner, Bob called Jupiter.

"He ate an early dinner and went right out," Aunt Mathilda Jones said. "No, Bob, he didn't say where."

By bedtime, Jupiter still hadn't called either Bob or Pete.

Where was Jupiter?

4 · Jupiter Finds the Key

The next morning Pete waited until after his breakfast. When Jupiter still hadn't called, the Second Investigator phoned Bob.

"He hasn't called me, either," Bob said.

They decided to bike over to the salvage yard before school. Headquarters was empty, so they went across the street to the Jones house.

Uncle Titus was out front tinkering with one of his pickup trucks. "Nope, sorry, boys, but Jupiter went out very early. Some important errand, he said. Hardly ate a smidgen of breakfast!"

"We'll have to find him in our first class," Bob decided.

"If he shows up," Pete said ominously.

The boys hurried to school and into their classroom. Jupiter wasn't there! They looked at each other nervously as the teacher called for order. Suddenly Jupiter came panting into the room, grinning at his chums. Bob and Pete had no chance to talk to him until lunch, and then only for a moment—Jupiter had to attend a lunch-hour meeting of the Science Club, of which he was president. He spoke to them hurriedly:

"I've got it! The key. Meet at Headquarters after school!"

Bob and Pete finished one class later than Jupiter on

Fridays. Burning with curiosity, they rode straight to the salvage yard. They crawled through Tunnel Two and up into the trailer. Jupiter was already there.

"Rhyming slang!" he announced.

He sat at the office desk surrounded by sheets of paper covered with writing.

"Huh?" Pete said. "What slang?"

"Rhyming," Jupiter crowed. "Something each of you said last night gave me the flash. Pete asked about Cockneys, and Bob said perhaps what the riddles *sounded* like was important. That made me think of rhyming slang. But I wasn't sure, so I checked it out, and I was right!"

"But what *is* rhyming slang, Jupe?" Bob asked.

"A very special slang in which a word, or the last word in a short phrase, rhymes with whatever word you really mean. The true meaning of the rhyming word doesn't matter—it just has to sound like the word in question. For example, you could call *snow* the *fall and throw*. See—snow and throw?"

"You mean," Pete said doubtfully, "if I was talking about *baseball*, I could call it, maybe, *throw the ball?*"

"Not quite. You'd never use the same word—not *ball* if you were rhyming *baseball*. You could call it *down the wall* or *short and tall*, or something."

"I get it!" Bob said. "But what's rhyming slang got to do with Cockneys or old Dingo? Wait, his dad was a Cockney!"

"And he was Australian. The Cockneys invented the slang, and took it to Australia. They still use it to fool people."

"Just like Dingo's riddles," Pete said.

Jupiter nodded. "I went to our library, and to Los Angeles, and looked up all the books on rhyming slang." He picked up a copy of the riddles. "First, *apples and pears* are—*stairs!*"

"Stairs?" Pete gaped. "Wow, I'd never have guessed that."

"No one else will, either." Jupiter chortled. "Now, *you and me* means *cup of tea. Trouble and strife* is Cockney for a *wife! Old Ned*, also called *Uncle Ned*, is a *bed.* See?"

Jupiter beamed at his friends.

"Then we've got it solved?" Pete said.

"Oh, no," Jupiter replied, shaking his head almost happily. "It's not that easy. Old Dingo was tricky. Only *some* of the clues are rhyming slang. Others we'll have to solve when we get to where the rhymes send us."

"But we've got all the rhymes?" Bob asked.

"Well, no," Jupiter said, a little uneasily. "I couldn't find them all, and rhyming slangers sometimes make up new ones."

"Then how do people know what they mean?" Bob insisted.

"By what the slanger is talking about in general, Bob," Jupiter explained. "We'll know what Dingo meant by where the clues lead us, and by what we find there. For instance, *apples and pears* means *stairs.* When we find some stairs, we should find something near them that rhymes with the next clue in the riddle—*the Lady from Bristol.*"

"Then," Bob said, "let's get started! We already know

that *where the wild dog lives* means Dingo's house. Next comes *bottle and stopper*. What's that?"

"Gosh," Pete said, "is that a rhyme we don't know?"

Jupiter's eyes twinkled. "No, that one is in all the books! I saved it for last. It's a simple one. Every convict would know—"

"Convict?" Bob said, his eyes wide. "*Copper!* A cop!"

"Exactly!" Jupiter said. "We look for a policeman somewhere near old Dingo's house."

"Then what are we waiting for?" Pete exclaimed. "Let's go!"

Jupiter gathered up his notes and told the others to collect their walkie-talkies—just in case they should start hunting in earnest after seeing the Townes. As Pete lifted up the trap door, the telephone suddenly rang. Jupiter grabbed it and answered hurriedly:

"The Three Investigators! I'm sorry, we're going out!"

A muffled voice filled the trailer from the speaker-phone. "It would be better if you did not go out. This is a warning. Do not meddle in other people's business. You could be hurt!"

There was a *click,* and then silence.

Bob swallowed hard. "That was a woman, Jupe, wasn't it?" he said shakily.

"I'm not sure," Jupiter said. "The voice was muffled. I *think* it was a woman—and the accent was English!"

"Winifred Percival!" Bob said.

"But we never talked to her," Pete pointed out. "How could she know us? How'd she get our phone number? The Townes wouldn't tell her."

"If it wasn't Miss Percival," Jupiter said, "who was it? Someone we don't know? Perhaps someone from Australia?"

"Maybe Mrs. Towne can tell us," Bob said.

The other two nodded uneasily. They went outside and mounted their bikes. As they rode toward the front entrance of the junkyard, they saw a figure in the distance through the yard gates. A man was standing in the shadow of some large bushes across the street from the salvage yard—an enormous man with a bright red tie who seemed to be smiling. Then he was gone! He seemed to vanish without even moving. The boys stared at each other.

"Was . . . was someone really there?" Pete asked.

"Do you suppose he was watching for us?" added Bob.

"Maybe," said Jupe. "Maybe not. He could have been someone just out taking a walk."

"Then where did he go?" cried Pete.

"Probably right down the street," answered Jupiter firmly. "The sun is so bright we could have missed him among all the shadows." He peered up and down the block. "Come on, there's no one there now. Let's go! We've got riddles to solve and a fortune to find."

"Sure," Pete said, "but I'd feel better if we had about a dozen bottles and stoppers around!"

They all laughed—nervously!

5· The Bottle and Stopper

As the boys rode up to Mrs. Towne's cottage, they grinned at each other. The scene at Dingo's place was even more comical than yesterday's—for opposite reasons. Policemen stood around with nothing to do. The few remaining treasure hunters kicked angrily at bottles and glowered as if they knew they'd been fooled but didn't quite know how!

In the cottage living room, Mrs. Towne told Billy to get Cokes for the boys, and Roger Callow smiled.

"You may be stumped, boys," the lawyer said, "but so is everyone else. Are they ever angry! You'd think *we* had robbed *them!*"

Pete blurted out, "Jupe's not stumped anymore!"

"See!" Billy cried as he came back into the room. "I told you we'd solve it."

"You know where the gemstones are?" Callow asked.

"No," Jupiter said, "but I think we've found the key to the riddles—part of it, anyway. Mrs. Towne, did old Dingo know some special policeman? Did he perhaps have a friend in the police?"

"My goodness, no! He hated policemen," Mrs. Towne said.

"A policeman?" Roger Callow said. "How does a policeman fit in with bottles and billabongs and pear trees?"

The boys drank their Cokes while Jupiter explained about rhyming slang.

"I've never heard of it," Callow said. "Have you, Nelly?"

"No, but I'm not Australian or English," Mrs. Towne said. "Perhaps Winifred and Cecil have. They're English."

"I doubt it," Jupiter decided. "They wouldn't associate with Cockneys."

Billy said eagerly, "Mr. Dillon and Granddad talked funny like that sometimes! I'll bet we've solved it."

"I'm sure of it," Jupiter declared. He spread out his copy of the will. "Let's analyze the riddles. First:

Where the wild dog lives, the bottle and stopper show the way to the billabong.

"*Where the wild dog lives* isn't rhyming slang; it just means Dingo's house, his land. The books agree that *bottle and stopper* is Cockney for a *copper*, a policeman. A *billabong* is Australian for a stream or water hole. So the first riddle tells us to come here and find a policeman who will know a special stream or pond!"

Callow exclaimed, "Nelly, you must know of a policeman!"

"But I don't, Roger! You know Dingo hated policemen."

Jupiter said, "There must be one, but let's go on:

Above the apples and pears all alone the Lady from Bristol rides from a friend.

"Now *apples and pears* are *stairs*. We don't know what *the Lady from Bristol* is yet. And *rides from a friend* doesn't sound like a rhyme; it must be some other kind of clue."

"So that riddle," Bob summed up, "tells us that around the special stream mentioned in Riddle One we should find some stairs, and above them, by itself, something that rhymes with *the Lady from Bristol* and gives a clue to a friend."

"Gee," Pete groaned, "that's not so easy."

"The clues must be taken step by step," Jupiter declared. "Maybe it's not the friend, but the *ride* from a friend that gives us the lead to the next riddle:

> *At the tenth ball of twine, you and me*
> *see our handsome mug ahead.*"

Jupiter scowled. "They get harder as they go along, I'm afraid. *You and me* is Cockney for a *cup of tea,* whatever that means, but I couldn't find *ball of twine,* and *see our handsome mug ahead* can't be a rhyme. And the fourth riddle doesn't tell me anything yet:

> *One man's victim is another's darlin',*
> *follow the nose to the place.*

"If there's a rhyme in that one, I don't see it."

Mrs. Towne said, "If *you and me* is a *cup of tea,* perhaps the *handsome mug* is some special tea cup somewhere."

"Yes, that could be it," Jupiter agreed.

"But," Bob said, "Dingo says *our* mug, not *the* mug or *his* mug. And in Riddle Four, why does he say *the* nose instead of *your* nose?"

"I don't know, Records," Jupiter admitted. "But I'm sure there's a reason. Now, take the fifth riddle:

Where men buy their trouble and strife,
get out if you can.

"*Trouble and strife* is slang for *wife,* but Dingo says *buy* a wife. Could that be something Australian, Mrs. Towne? Didn't the settlers buy wives from England?"

"In a way, Jupiter," Mrs. Towne said. "Whole shiploads of women were sent out for the settlers to choose wives from."

Jupiter nodded. "Well, that might fit in somehow, and *get out if you can* might then mean escaping marriage. But that doesn't make much sense. Well, on to the sixth riddle:

In the posh Queen's old Ned, be bright
and natural and the prize is yours.

"The *old Ned* is a *bed,* and *posh* is just an ordinary word for *elegant.* So it looks as if the last riddle says we'll find the gems in some elegant Queen's bed!"

Roger Callow shook his head. "What Queen? What bed? In some museum, perhaps?"

"Possibly," Jupiter answered, "but we shouldn't worry about the last riddle now. I'm convinced that we won't guess any clue until we've solved the one before it."

"So first we find the *bottle and stopper*," Bob said, "who knows about some stream or water hole—a billabong."

Pete said, "Maybe Dingo liked to swim somewhere special, or get water, or go fishing, or—"

"Fishing!" Billy cried. "Mom! Granddad used to fish in the county park next door with Deputy Lopez!"

"A deputy sheriff?" Bob said. "He's a policeman! A county policeman!"

"Of course," Roger Callow said. "At the park substation!"

Suddenly Pete whispered, "Jupe! On the street!"

They all looked out and saw a man leaning against a blue car parked under the trees. A giant of a man!

"Another curiosity-seeker, I suppose," Roger Callow said.

"Maybe," Jupiter said uneasily, and told him about the giant man they had seen near the salvage yard.

Roger Callow walked to the door. "We'd better see about this!"

The boys watched the lawyer start off toward the street. The giant man got into his car and drove off. Callow came back.

"A sightseer, I'm sure," the lawyer said. "There have been dozens of them."

The Investigators started for the door and their bikes. Billy came after them.

"I'll work with you, too, fellows!"

"You'll do no such thing, Billy Towne!" his mother said.

Pete agreed. "We can't solve a case and babysit, too."

"Who's a baby!" Billy cried. "You take that back!"

"You'd only be in our way, Billy," Jupiter decided.

The small boy stormed into his room, yelling, "I'll show you all!"

The boys went outside and got on their bikes. Jupiter patted his pocket to make sure he had his walkie-talkie and said, "Now we're getting somewhere! Let's go, fellows!"

Out on the street they turned left, away from town, and headed for the entrance to the county park. Along their right side was a woody area, followed by a large shopping center. Along their left stretched the Botanical Gardens, a carefully landscaped area with many rare and beautiful plantings. Behind the gardens the county park rose into the foothills of the coastal mountains. From Dingo's street, a road wound through the gardens and park to the hilly residential area beyond.

The Investigators turned into the park road and pedaled up a rise. They heard a car turn in behind them, then accelerate. Pete looked back and let out a squawk. The car was right on top of them! And it wasn't swerving to pass them!

"Off the road!" yelled Pete, and headed his bike into the drainage ditch. A red sports car roared past, grazing Bob's bike and knocking it over. Bob leaped clear and landed in the ditch with a thud. Pete looked after the disappearing car, saw a laughing face, and yelled again.

"Skinny Norris! Trying to get even with us for fooling him last night!"

"Skinny never learns," Jupe said as he helped Bob out of the ditch and made sure he was all right. "Skinny always goes too far, and that makes him dangerous. We'll have to keep an eye out for him."

The boys went on up the road a short way and found the deputy's substation. No one was there. They walked into the Botanical Gardens and looked around. Bob pointed ahead.

"Look at the trees, fellows! And the pond!"

A hurricane seemed to have hit the gardens! The apple and pear trees that grew around the duck pond were ragged and broken. Branches lay all over the ground and in the pond itself. Usually dozens of geese and ducks could be seen feeding in the water, but there wasn't one bird around today.

Avoiding the many holes that had been dug in the ground, the boys wandered through the destruction.

"Looks like another mob of searchers came here," concluded Pete. He leaned over and picked up a tree branch.

"You three! Stand right there!" an angry voice called.

They whirled. Behind them, a small, dark-faced man in a sheriff's uniform glared at them.

"You're all under arrest!"

6·A Dangerous Prank

Jupiter remained calm. "Are you Deputy Lopez, Officer?"

"I am," the dark man growled. "*Diablo!* I have had enough of you vandals and that dead man's riddle! You I am arresting!"

"But," Bob protested, "we're not—!"

Jupiter said quietly, "If you'll notice, Deputy Lopez, the branch my friend is holding has wilted leaves on it. It was broken much earlier, probably yesterday. We just arrived, and we broke nothing."

"Well," Deputy Lopez said suspiciously, "if you are not here for Dingo's treasure, why are you?"

"We did come to find—" Jupiter began.

"Ah!" the deputy cried. "So I am right!"

"But," Jupiter went on firmly, "the pond and the trees have nothing to do with the treasure. The mob that ruined them made a mistake. We're not part of that mob. We were hired by Mrs. Towne to find Dingo's fortune for her."

"Hired?" Deputy Lopez said, still suspicious.

"We're detectives!" Pete said.

Jupiter held out their card from Chief Reynolds. "Chief Reynolds will vouch for us. You can call him or Mrs. Towne."

Deputy Lopez read the card and shrugged.

"It's the Chief's signature all right. So you're The Three Investigators?" He scratched his head. "Then you think that old Dingo really did hide something? It's not just a joke?"

"We're sure he hid something," Jupiter said, "and we need your help."

"My help?" Deputy Lopez said. "*Caramba!* How can I help?"

"By telling us where the billabong is!" Pete declared.

Deputy Lopez stared, "Billabong? What is a billabong?"

"A water hole, or stream," Jupiter said. "You and Dingo used to go fishing somewhere in the park?"

"Sure, up in the old reservoir. Where they dammed up Ynez Creek for water, before we got our water from over the mountains. It's not used anymore except for fishing, and bad fishing at that—too shallow except now in spring. Most of the old feeder creeks are cemented up for flood control, but the main creek still runs. There's an old houseboat up there that we fished from."

"Can you tell us the way, sir?" Bob asked eagerly.

"Sure, it's easy. The road goes right up by it. It's just below the main bus stop for the park."

He explained how to find the old reservoir, and the boys thanked him and ran back to their bikes. Pedaling hard, they followed the winding road up through the park, and saw the old dam ahead, high above them to the right. Water was pouring over it in a heavy stream twenty feet wide. The boys kept climbing till they were on a level with the dam. Here a dirt road led off to Ynez Creek, while the main park road looped past the old reservoir and continued up the mountain above it.

The boys turned down the dirt road and soon saw a small houseboat moored to the near bank of the creek. Here, just before the dam, the creek was about thirty feet wide. It was full from the spring rains and ran swiftly past the houseboat.

"Well," Bob said as he dropped his bike on the bank, "this takes care of Riddle One. The *bottle and stopper* has shown us the way to the *billabong!*"

"Now for Riddle Two," Pete said. "*Above the apples and pears all alone.* We need some stairs—and there they are!"

A steep flight of wooden stairs—almost a ladder—led from the main deck of the houseboat to a deck on top of its flat-roofed cabin. Pete led the rush aboard the houseboat, across the single board that served as a gangplank, and up the stairs. The roof deck, which was surrounded by a railing, was littered with boxes and old lumber and rusted bait cans.

"Look for something that rhymes with *Lady from Bristol*," Jupiter said. "Something that rhymes, and stands all by itself."

The three boys began to search energetically through everything on the deck. They turned over boxes, looked into tin cans, and picked up the lumber. But they found nothing! Jupiter even lifted up some loose deck boards. There was only empty space underneath.

"Gosh," Pete said, "I don't see anything that rhymes with *Bristol.*"

"But it has to be here!" Jupiter insisted. "I *know* we're on the right track. Lopez is a policeman, he knew

Dingo, and this is the only stream around. It *must* be the billabong!"

"Maybe Dingo meant that you can see something on shore from up here," Bob said.

They stood at the railing and let their eyes roam over the wooded landscape on both sides of the dammed-up creek. The mountain rose on the far side, and a dry, cemented feeder channel went out of sight up its slope. They saw nothing that could possibly rhyme with *Bristol*. Until . . .

"You think . . . *whistle?*" Jupiter said, and pointed to the small air-horn on the roof of the houseboat's forward wheelhouse.

"Well," Pete said slowly, "you could call that a whistle, except it's usually called a horn on a small boat. And, gee, *whistle* isn't a very good rhyme for *Bristol,* and what does it point to, Jupe?"

"It points straight up," Bob said.

"I guess you're right," Jupiter said. "What we want should rhyme exactly with *Lady from Bristol*, and it should point to something that fits the next clue, *rides from a friend.* Maybe we've made some mistake and come to the wrong—"

They all heard the noise! From somewhere below them came a thump—like a heavy board hitting dirt!

The three boys rushed to the railing on the land side. Skinny Norris stood below on the bank. He sneered up at them.

"Thanks again—for the right answer this time," the nasty youth said. "I heard it all, and I know where the stairs are. This time *I* solve the case!" He laughed. "And you're not going anywhere for a while! Bon voyage, creeps!"

"Jupe!" Bob cried, "The houseboat's loose!"

The gangplank lay on the shore, and the lines that had tied the houseboat fore and aft trailed in the water! The boys tumbled down the stairs to the main deck. It was too late! The houseboat was ten feet from shore and drifting farther away.

Pete clenched his fists. "Skinny Norris, you—"

"Have a nice sail, fellows," Skinny yelled. "You'll drift ashore in a couple of hours!"

Skinny ran off down the dirt road, looking very pleased with himself.

"Wait till I get ahold of him!" threatened Pete.

"Guys!" Bob suddenly cried. "The dam!"

They all looked forward. The houseboat was drifting downstream and gathering speed rapidly. A low roar grew louder. Straight ahead the racing creek swept over the edge of the dam in a deep mass of roaring water!

7 · Pete Takes Over

The houseboat swept on!

"Swim, fellows!" Jupiter cried.

"No!" Pete commanded. "Stand still, both of you!"

Jupiter and Bob both froze.

"The current's too fast. We'd be swept over for sure," Pete explained urgently. "Quick, on top!"

Jupiter and Bob followed Pete up to the top deck. The dam was coming closer every second!

"Hurry," Pete instructed, "push the boxes, lumber, everything heavy toward the stern!"

Puffing and panting, the boys shoved everything on the top deck toward the rear of the houseboat. Just as they finished they heard a grating sound, and the houseboat's forward motion slowed. Jupiter stammered:

"We–we're on the dam!"

Ahead, there was nothing but empty space and mist rising from far below, where the water crashed down on rocks. Bob swallowed, his face pale. Jupiter closed his eyes as the houseboat hung on the edge of the dam and tilted!

"Are we . . . are we . . . over?" Jupiter quavered.

The houseboat shuddered, slipped ahead—and then stopped! It rested on the edge of the dam with the water pouring over on either side.

"Good. We're caught on the dam," Pete said quietly.

Jupiter opened his eyes and started forward.

"No!" Pete shouted. "Don't move!"

Jupiter stopped dead.

"The houseboat's stuck by the stern," Pete explained. "We've got just enough weight at the rear—with ourselves."

Almost afraid to breathe, the three boys looked around. They were halfway over the dam, and some ten feet from shore on both sides. They were stuck in the exact center!

"What do we do now?" Bob said.

Pete considered the situation calmly. "We can't swim or float ashore on a box. We can't jump it. There aren't any tree branches overhead that we could reach. And if we make any sudden movements, over we go."

Jupiter's voice was panicky. "Then what *can* we do, Second?"

"First, keep calm, Jupe," Pete said. "I saw some rope down below. I think I can lasso that big stump over there on the bank. Then we can cross by the rope. Bob, you're the lightest. Go down for the rope."

Bob nodded and started for the stairs. The houseboat creaked and tilted forward!

"Not that way!" Pete cried. "Climb over the rail here at the stern, Bob! We've got to keep our weight at the rear."

Bob nodded, climbed over the rail, and swung gently down to the lower deck. In a moment he handed up a long coil of rope. Pete made a lasso at one end of it, positioned himself slowly, and threw the lasso toward shore. It fell three feet short of the stump.

Pete pulled the rope back and tried again. This time the lasso hit the stump—and slipped off! The houseboat teetered, forcing the boys to hang onto the railing for balance. Jupiter glanced upstream—and paled.

"P–Pete! A big log! If it hits us, we'll go over!"

Pete calmly eyed the big log floating down the creek toward the houseboat. He nodded, recoiled the rope, and threw again. The lasso caught! Carefully, Pete drew the line tight and tied it to the railing of the upper deck.

"Bob, you go first," he said.

Below, Bob moved over to stand under the rope, reached up for it, and gently swung hand over hand along it. Moments later he stood safely on shore! He quickly pushed the lasso down farther on the tree stump and held it in place.

"Go, Jupe," Pete said.

Jupiter hesitated. He wasn't as strong as his companions and wondered if he could make it across. Then he saw the big log coming closer. He swallowed and swung out over the rushing creek. His greater weight pulled the rope down so that his feet dragged in the water, and his shoulders ached with every swing forward. But soon he, too, was stumbling ashore.

The boat teetered ominously with both Bob and Jupiter's weight gone from the stern. And the big log was almost up to the houseboat! Pete didn't wait. He grabbed the line and almost slid across. Just as his feet touched land, the big log struck the boat.

With the weight of the boys gone, the houseboat tilted—and slid over the dam to crash and burst apart on the rocks below! On shore, the boys shivered as the crash echoed up and down the canyon.

"Wow," Bob finally said.

Pete scowled angrily. "That Skinny! He's dangerous!"

"Skinny," said Jupiter, taking a deep breath, "has a head start on us! He said he knows where the stairs are! Come on!"

The First Investigator's eyes were hot and bright. The danger past, his mind was on the puzzle again immediately!

"The stairs have to be around here somewhere," he said. "We'll split up and search. Keep in contact with the walkie-talkies. If you spot any stairs, report!"

They began to search along Ynez Creek, crossing to the far side on a footbridge above the reservoir. Up and down they went, keeping in touch with their walkie-talkies, but they found nothing.

"Something's wrong, fellows," Jupiter finally said into his walkie-talkie.

"You're not kidding!" answered Pete.

"Jupe, are you sure we've solved Riddle One correctly?" asked Bob. "Are you *positive* that a billabong is a stream?"

"Of course . . ." Jupe hesitated. "Wait! I never did check that word in the dictionary. Maybe it has a more specific meaning than I remembered. Is anyone near a telephone?"

"I think there's one down near the deputy's substation," answered Pete. "Do you want me to ride down? I'm near our bikes."

"Do that," ordered Jupe. "Call the library and ask the librarian if she'll read you the definition of billabong. Hurry!"

Pete clicked off. He was gone a long time. The sun sank lower and lower in the sky. Jupe was just thinking that it would be dark soon when Pete's voice suddenly came over the walkie-talkie.

"Jupe! Bob! Are you there?"

"Here, Second. What have you found out?" demanded Jupe.

"I'll read you the definitions. Billabong means several different things. 'One. A branch of a river flowing away from the main stream but leading to no other body of water; a blind or dead-end channel.' "

"That's no help," commented Bob. "We haven't seen anything like that."

"Hold on. Here's another. 'Two. A creek bed holding water only in the rainy season; a dried-up water course.' "

"That's it!" Jupiter exclaimed. "There's that cemented feeder creek upstream from the dam! It has water in it only after a rain. Pete, meet us there! Over and out!"

A few minutes later Bob and Jupe arrived at the mouth of the feeder stream on the far side of Ynez Creek. The dry cement channel curved up the slope of the brush-covered mountain. They climbed up along the channel slowly, one on either side, all the way to the end.

"Nothing," Bob said, unbelieving. "No stairs anywhere!"

"There must be," Jupiter insisted. "I'm sure this is old Dingo's billabong. Come on."

They retraced their steps in the fading light. Partway down, they heard Pete yelling at them from the other side of Ynez Creek.

"There, guys!" Pete was pointing downstream, to their left.

"Where?" said Bob. "I don't see anything."

"The stairs must be placed so that you can't see them from up close or right below," said Jupe. "Come on!"

The stocky boy plunged into the bushes and trees covering the slope and scrambled across the side of the mountain. Bob followed. In minutes they saw an old flight of wooden stairs among the brush. Bits of it gleamed gold where the setting sun came through the trees. The steps came only halfway down the mountain.

"A flood must have washed away the lower part," said Jupiter. "Or maybe it just fell apart. These stairs are in pretty bad shape."

Pete came panting up the mountain and joined them. "Boy, that Dingo is tricky! You can't see these stairs from the creek at all! I just got a glimpse from the road."

"Let's hope Skinny's eyes aren't as good as yours," said Jupe. "Let's go!"

The boys raced up the rickety old steps, which ended at a small, open meadow on the top of the mountain. The main park road passed by on the far side. There was a bus stop some fifty yards away—and there was a small bronze statue in the meadow.

"Jupe!" cried Bob. "The statue!"

It was a small statue of a cowboy, standing on a granite pedestal. The cowboy was aiming his pistol.

"A *pistol*," Pete cried. "*The Lady from Bristol*—and alone!"

"Where does the pistol point?" Jupiter demanded.

Pete climbed up on the pedestal and bent to sight along the pistol. He blinked and slowly shook his head.

"It doesn't point at anything, Jupe."

Bob climbed up and sighted. "It just points at trees, Jupe."

Jupiter stared at the base of the small statue where it rested on the granite pedestal.

"Hmmm," he said, "the statue isn't fixed on the pedestal. It's just kept on by a pin at the center—so it can move during all our small earthquakes. It's loose, and it's been moved!"

"Moved?" Pete frowned. "You mean by an earthquake?"

Jupiter shook his head. "No, the marks are fresh, and there's even stone dust. It's been moved very recently."

"Skinny!" Pete groaned.

"Who else?" Jupiter answered grimly. "He found the statue, and he rotated it so we don't know what it pointed to!"

"Then how will we ever solve the next clue?" Bob asked.

"By finding Skinny!" Jupiter declared.

As they turned to go back to the stairs, a shadow moved in the twilight among the trees—a quick shadow that ran off toward the park road.

"Someone was watching us!" Bob said.

"After him!" Jupiter urged.

They ran through the trees. On the road ahead a car started. By the time the boys reached the road, the car was already distant.

"Did anyone recognize the car?" Jupiter asked.

"No," Pete said, "but it wasn't Skinny's!"

They went back down the mountain, crossed Ynez Creek on the footbridges, and picked up their bikes. As they rode off in the dusk, Bob said:

"Jupe, maybe it was that giant man again?"

"The shadow was too small," Jupiter said. "No, someone else is interested in what we're doing, fellows."

Pete looked nervously into the shadows along the road, remembering the telephone warning they'd had.

"Well, where do we look for Skinny?" asked Bob. "Not that he'll ever tell us where that pistol pointed."

"No, he won't," agreed Jupe. "But he might start boasting, the way he always does, and let something drop. First, let's see if he's at home. We're so late for dinner, a few more minutes won't matter."

But Skinny wasn't home. His mother said he was out with his father for the evening.

"Now what?" said Bob.

"We outflank him!" said Jupiter. "I don't think he'll have time to go treasure hunting tonight, but starting tomorrow we'll have to watch his every move! He heard us talking on the houseboat so he knows about the rhyming slang. Even Skinny could figure out the riddles now!"

"Gosh, Jupe," said Pete. "We can't keep Skinny covered every minute. We haven't got a car."

"We don't need one," announced Jupe. "We've got something better—the Ghost-to-Ghost Hookup!"

8·Unexpected Visitors

Several hours later Pete Crenshaw put down the family phone and announced, "There! That finishes my calls for the Ghost-to-Ghost."

"Calls for ghosts?" said his dad. "Are you feeling all right?"

"Not ghosts, Dad, the Ghost-to-Ghost Hookup. Remember? It's Jupe's invention for finding something or someone fast. We each call five different friends, tell them what we're looking for, and ask them to pass the message on to five of their friends, who then call five of *their* friends, and so on. It grows geometrically, Jupe says—like a chain letter. We get every kid in Rocky Beach, almost, to help us! Anyway, it sure works."

Mr. Crenshaw looked dazed. "I can imagine."

Pete smiled to himself. Skinny Norris was fixed, for sure. The Three Investigators had put out a bulletin for any information on Skinny's whereabouts tomorrow. Just about every kid in town would be keeping an eye out for Skinny's red sports car and sneering face. Anyone who saw him would call the Investigators at Headquarters.

The next morning Pete got up early, even though it was Saturday, and phoned Jupiter before breakfast.

"Any calls from the Ghost-to-Ghost?"

"Two, Second," Jupiter answered. "One person saw

the wrong car, and the other spotted Skinny's car in the Norris driveway."

"Well, we know he's still at home," Pete said. "I'll be over right after breakfast."

Since he was in a hurry, Pete ate only three eggs and six slices of bacon, and ran out the moment he'd finished his milk. He biked rapidly to The Jones Salvage Yard and crawled up into Headquarters. Jupiter was there alone.

"Bob has to do some chores for his mother," the First Investigator said. "I've been working on the riddles. Did you notice how often old Dingo uses a word you don't expect? I mean, in the riddle we're working on now, the *Lady from Bristol* rides *from* a friend."

"So?" Pete asked.

"The phrase *rides from* a friend is rather odd, considering that the pistol pointed *to* something. Why not say rides *to a friend?*"

"Gee, I don't know."

"Then, remember what Bob said earlier? How in Riddle Three old Dingo wrote *our* handsome mug, and in Riddle Four he wrote follow *the* nose, and in Riddle Five he said *buy* a wife?"

"You mean he should have said to follow *your* nose, and to see *my* mug or *the* mug?" Pete said. "And who *buys* a wife?"

Jupiter nodded vigorously. "I'm convinced that those words are all very important. There's something extra tricky about them."

"If you ask me," Pete sighed, "the whole crazy will is too tricky. Dingo sure didn't make it easy."

Jupiter's eyes shone. "And I'm sure that means there *is* a hidden fortune! Dingo wanted it hard to find."

"He succeeded, all right!" Pete said. "We'd better find Skinny—"

"Pete! Jupe!" The call came faintly into the trailer.

"That sounds like Bob," Pete said.

Jupiter went over to the See-All—the crude but efficient periscope that he had rigged up so they could see over the junk piled up around the trailer. The See-All consisted of a length of stove pipe with mirrors installed at angles in it. It rose through the roof in one corner of the trailer. Jupiter rotated the See-All and located Bob.

"He's coming toward the workshop," Jupe said. "Somebody's with him! Let's go outside. Tunnel Two won't be safe—use Door Four."

Door Four was a sliding panel in the back wall of the trailer. It opened onto a secret narrow corridor that led through high junk piles to the back of the yard. Pete and Jupe hurried along the corridor and circled around to the workshop area in front. Bob was waiting for them there—with Winifred Percival!

"What the—?" Pete began.

"Ah!" an English voice said, "now we are all here."

Pete and Jupiter whirled. Cecil Percival had just appeared in the entrance to the workshop. The fat nephew of Dingo Towne held a heavy black walking stick—and blocked the way out.

"What do you two want!" Pete demanded hotly.

"Tut, tut, my lad," Cecil chided, his fat face severe. "You American children have such shocking manners!

We wish simply to have a talk, nothing more. Isn't that so, Winny dear?"

"For the moment," the thin woman said ominously.

"Now, now, we mustn't alarm the boys. We merely wish them to understand the true facts, eh?" Cecil said.

Jupiter said, "You've tried to alarm us already, haven't you? With that anonymous telephone warning yesterday."

"Warning?" Cecil said blandly. "Whatever can you mean? If someone threatened you, my young friends, I suggest you ask Mr. Callow about it."

"We're not your friends!" Pete snapped.

"Ah, but we want you to be," Cecil said. "You have a mistaken impression of us. Your minds have been poisoned by Nelly Towne and Roger Callow."

"Our mother, the sister of Marcus, was his partner years ago," Winifred said, her skinny face angry. "He stole her rightful share of his money! It belongs to us now!"

"You're working for the wrong people," Cecil said. "We should like you to work for us. We'd pay you much better."

"We don't—!" Bob began angrily.

Jupiter broke in, "How much better, sir?"

"Why," Cecil said quickly, "say ten percent of the whole fortune. That could be a king's ransom, boys."

"Hmmmmm," Jupiter mused, "very generous."

Pete and Bob watched their stocky leader in surprise.

"We just find the gems for you?" Jupiter asked.

"Find them, tell no one else, and give them to us!"

"Tell no one else," Jupiter said sharply. "So you can

steal them! You *know* you don't have a legal claim to Dingo's fortune. Well, we have a client—the real heirs—and detectives can't work for two clients."

Cecil's face darkened. Winifred muttered under her breath. The man's fleshy face shook with anger, and he raised his heavy stick menacingly.

"Then you'll tell us what you've learned!" Cecil said. "We know you're on the right track, we know all about the rhyming slang, and we saw you at that creek with the other young scamp! You'll tell us what you know!"

"So it was you watching us at the statue!" Bob exclaimed.

"Statue?" Winifred said. "What statue?"

Jupiter said, "You didn't see Skinny . . . the other boy, near a statue in the Botanical Gardens? You didn't see what he did?"

"We saw no statue," Cecil said, "but we saw you all at the creek. We followed the other boy, but he eluded us. Now you—"

"How do you know about the rhyming slang?" Jupiter went on. "How did you know we're working for the Townes in the first place?"

Cecil laughed. "Billy Towne is a foolish boy. He was so angry at us, so intent on proving us wrong, that he blurted out everything about you and your discovery that Dingo used rhyming slang."

"Terribly vulgar, that slang," Winifred said. "We—"

"Enough, Winifred!" Cecil suddenly roared. "Now, I will ask the questions! Tell us what you know, and be quick!"

"No, sir," Jupiter said, "we won't tell you."

"We'll tell you nothing!" Pete echoed.

"Then," Cecil said darkly, "we'll have to see that you tell no one else."

The fat man raised his heavy walking stick and stepped toward the boys. His small eyes glittered.

"We'll just keep you somewhere for a time. Somewhere out of our way until we solve the riddles ourselves!"

The boys shrank back as Cecil and Winifred advanced.

"What's going on here!" a booming voice demanded.

Aunt Mathilda Jones stood in the workshop entrance behind the Percivals. Cecil whirled, his stick raised threateningly.

"Stand back, madam!" the fat man warned.

Aunt Mathilda turned purple. She strode to Cecil, grabbed the stick, and whacked him on the head. Cecil howled and stumbled back. Winifred jumped toward Aunt Mathilda.

"I wouldn't come closer!" Aunt Mathilda warned. Winifred stopped. Aunt Mathilda threw the heavy stick out across the salvage yard. "Now you two leave here right now!"

Hans, one of Uncle Titus Jones's big Bavarian helpers, appeared not far away and gazed inquiringly at the workshop.

"And stay away," Aunt Mathilda snapped.

Cecil looked toward Hans, then nodded angrily at Winifred. The two of them stalked away with the boys' laughter ringing in their ears. Aunt Mathilda eyed the boys.

"Well," she said, "what was that all about?"

Jupiter explained who the Percivals were, and what they had wanted. Aunt Mathilda snorted.

"If you ask me, those treasure hunters are all crazy," she said. "Who ever heard of solving a dead man's riddle? Well, I don't expect those two will bother you again."

As she walked back to the junkyard office, the boys grinned at each other. No one tangled with Aunt Mathilda!

Suddenly the boys noticed that a red light over Jupe's workbench was flashing—the signal that the telephone inside Headquarters was ringing. They scrambled through Tunnel Two and Jupiter grabbed the phone.

"Thanks," he said after a moment, and hung up. "Skinny's been spotted at the bus depot!"

They hurried out to their bikes.

9 · A Ride from a Friend

Jupiter said, "We're being followed!"

They were a block from the bus depot in downtown Rocky Beach. Riding as fast as they could, they hadn't looked back until they were forced to stop for a traffic light.

"Where?" Bob said, glancing around. "I don't see anyone."

"He ducked behind a parked car," Jupiter said. "He's on a bike, wearing some weird hat and cape! Go up the side street!"

They turned right as the light changed and raced up the side street. Halfway along the block was an alley, which they skidded into. Crouching in the shadows behind some trash bins, they watched and waited.

The weird figure on the bike was coming up the street after them!

The small, thick shape looked like a hunchback bent over the handlebars. He wore a bulky black cape and an odd hat with a cap brim back and front! Pete whispered:

"It's like the hat Sherlock Holmes wore!"

"A deerstalker," Bob whispered back.

"Oh, no!" Jupiter cried, and stood up. "Billy Towne! What are you doing here?"

Startled, the little boy ran into a parked car and fell

off in a tangle of bike and cape. He struggled up, kicking at the cape, and stood as tall as he could.

"I'm helping you! I don't care what you say!"

"In that outfit?" Pete laughed.

"It's what a detective wears!" Billy cried defiantly.

"How did you find us?" Jupiter wanted to know.

"I followed you," Billy said proudly. "I got up early and watched the salvage yard. Boy, were the Percivals mad, huh? Why are you down here? Are you on a clue?"

"Never mind, Billy," said Jupe. "Come on everybody." He got on his bike and headed back to the intersection.

"Hey, where are we going?" called Billy as he pedaled hard to catch up.

"We're taking you home," said Jupiter wearily. "We can't be responsible for you and a case at the same time!"

"I don't want to go—"

A Jaguar turned up the side street and stopped. Roger Callow jumped out.

"So there you are, Billy! Your mother's very angry." Roger Callow smiled at the Investigators. "She guessed where he'd gone when he disappeared. It's a good thing you boys told Jupiter's aunt where you were headed or I'd never have found him."

"I won't go home!" Billy said. "I'm working with them!"

"Billy," Jupiter said, "the Percivals found out we're working for you, and they found out that rhyming slang is the key to the riddles. How do they know this?

Because *you* told them! The first rule of detective work, Billy, is never to talk unnecessarily. You made a very bad mistake."

"I'm sorry, Jupiter. Really I am. I just got mad when they said nasty things about my mom. I won't make any more mistakes. I promise!"

"I'm sorry, too, Billy," Jupiter said. "But you're hurting us more than you're helping. You'd better go with Mr. Callow."

Downcast, Billy wheeled his bike slowly to Roger Callow's car. As the lawyer loaded it in, he asked:

"Are you making any progress, boys?"

"We sure are," Pete boasted. "We'll solve Riddle Two soon."

"Good. I'm already busy in court about the wills, and the sooner we find the gems the better. Thank goodness most of the fortune hunters have given up. Keep in close touch, boys."

"We will, sir," Bob said.

Callow drove off, with Billy looking unhappily back at The Three Investigators.

They biked on to the depot and found the boy who had called them. His name was Fred Merkle. He met them in a doorway next to the depot so that Skinny wouldn't see them.

"I found the car maybe an hour ago," Fred Merkle said. "Your guy's been riding buses all morning, the dispatcher told me. Two different routes already, and he's about to leave on a third!"

As if to confirm what Fred Merkle said, a bus came out of the depot and passed in front of the boys. They shrank back out of sight. Skinny sat in a front seat on the bus—with his face black as thunder!

"Gosh, Skinny sure looks mad," Pete said.

"I guess he can't find what he wants," said Fred Merkle. "I talked with the drivers of the two buses he already took, and they both say he asked if anything on their routes rhymed with *friend*. The drivers couldn't think of anything special." The boy grinned. "Well, I got to go. It was fun."

"We appreciate it, Fred," Jupiter said. "If we get a reward, we'll send you a share."

As the Ghost-to-Ghost helper left them on the sunny sidewalk, Pete was thinking hard.

"What *does* rhyme with friend?" the Second Investigator said. "*Dead end,* maybe?"

"Much too general, Second," Jupiter said.

"Jupe," Bob wondered, "what did that pistol on the statue point to that made Skinny come to the bus depot?"

"I believe that's obvious now, Bob," Jupiter declared. "The *Lady from Bristol* must have pointed toward the main bus stop in the county park. It was near the statue, you remember. With the word *ride* in the clue, even Skinny could figure out that the riddle had to mean a bus."

"But," Bob went on, "why come here? Why not catch the bus up in the park?"

"And why is Skinny riding around so much?" Pete added.

Jupiter reflected. "I think, fellows, there can be only one answer to both of those questions. Let's check the bus routes inside."

They went into the depot and looked up the routes.

"I thought so," Jupiter said. "There are three different buses that go to the main stop in the park!"

"Skinny doesn't know which route Dingo meant," Bob said.

"Neither do we!" Pete groaned.

Jupiter furrowed his brow. "He had to mean one special route, and somehow it has to lead us to Riddle Three. So something in Riddle Two must tell us."

The stocky leader took out his copy of the riddles:

"Above the apples and pears all alone
the Lady from Bristol rides from a friend."

Pete asked, "Does one of the route numbers rhyme with *friend?*"

"Route *ten* almost rhymes," Bob said, "but the rhyme ought to be exact. Jupe, in those rhyming-slang books, you didn't find *ride from a friend,* did you?"

"No, I didn't," Jupiter said. "So *friend* has to be an obscure or made-up bit of rhyming slang, or *not* a rhyming clue at all! I think this is one of old Dingo's tricks. He means this clue literally—the bus we want is a real one that he took to visit a real friend. A friend he saw regularly, I'll bet, so someone can tell who he visited! I think—"

Jupiter blinked and stopped talking. Winifred Percival stood in the depot in front of the boys! The skinny niece of old Dingo seemed almost scared.

"I think you're right, young man," she said, "and I

think I know who that friend is. Perhaps I can make amends."

Pete said, "Jupe, it's some kind of—"

"Trick?" Winifred said. She nodded. "I can't blame you for being suspicious. I can only say Cecil *made* me join him. He's a violent man. He scares me. But I must try to stop him, for his own good."

"Stop him?" Jupiter said warily.

"By making sure someone else solves the riddles and finds the treasure first! I returned to the salvage yard to apologize and offer my help to you, and your aunt was kind enough to send me here. I won't help Cecil any more, no matter what he threatens."

"Gosh," Pete said. "Would he *hurt* you, ma'am?"

"He's capable of anything." Winifred shivered. "That's why I must help you beat him. Will you let me? I don't know this friend's exact address, but I can take you there."

Jupiter frowned. "Who is this friend, Miss Percival?"

"Well . . . you're Jupiter, right? And you're Bob and Pete?"

The boys nodded, still watching her uncertainly.

She smiled. "Good. Well, Uncle Dingo played chess regularly with a certain Mr. Pollinger."

"Did he take a bus there, ma'am?" Pete asked.

"Yes, but I don't know which one."

"Well, where does Mr. Pollinger live?" asked Bob.

"Back in the hills beyond that park next to Dingo's house," answered Winifred.

Jupiter nodded. That was the area the three bus routes went into. "Mr. Pollinger might be the right friend," he said. "It's worth a try. How do we get there?"

Winifred Percival said, "It's rather too far for biking, boys. If you'd trust me, I could take you in my car. Of course, if you'd rather not, I'd understand."

"Well—" Jupiter hesitated.

"I think I can describe Mr. Pollinger's house well enough for you to find it," Winifred said, "or I'll ride the buses with you to prove I don't plan to kidnap you." She smiled.

The boys looked at each other.

"The car sure would save time," Pete said.

Jupiter came to a decision. "Time is vital. We accept your offer."

"Good," Winifred said. "My car is in the depot lot. You can leave your bikes there."

The boys made sure the car was empty before they got in, and sat alertly as Winifred drove out past the Botanical Gardens and the park to a rural area of small cottages scattered among the hills. After a while she pointed to a narrow side road and said, "Up there, I think, boys."

Jupiter and Pete relaxed as they went up the narrow road in the spring sunshine. The car stopped in front of a rustic cottage.

"This is it!" said Winifred Percival.

The boys piled out and looked around. It was a lovely spot, with birds singing everywhere.

Still a little wary, Bob called out, "Mr. Pollinger! Mr. Pollinger? Can we ask you about Mr. Marcus Towne?"

There was a pause, and then a quavery old voice

came from inside. "Who is it? Old Dingo, eh? Beat the scoundrel every game, I did! Well, come in, come in!"

The boys hurried inside, with Jupiter already talking:

"Sir, Dingo rode a bus here, didn't he? Did he ever say anything about the bus and *a ball of twine?*"

An old man stood at a bookcase on the far side of the room, his back to the boys. He turned slowly.

"Well, hello, you meddling young fools!"

He wasn't old, and he wasn't Mr. Pollinger! Cecil Percival brandished his heavy walking stick and laughed nastily at the boys. Behind them, Winifred Percival blocked the front door!

10 · A Reckless Driver

Winifred Percival snarled at The Three Investigators.

"You didn't really think I would give up what is ours, did you?"

Pete and Bob were too shocked to answer. Jupiter trembled with rage but held his tongue, waiting to see what would happen.

"An excellent job, my dear Winifred," Cecil said, and sneered at the boys.

Winifred laughed. "They're much too honest and eager. Anyone could fool them!"

"Inventing Mr. Pollinger was clever of us, eh?" crowed Cecil. The fat man rubbed his hands in glee.

"You—!" Pete began hotly.

"Temper, temper!" chided Cecil. "I told you little fools earlier that you were in the way. Not that Winifred and I don't appreciate your work so far. Not at all! But *we* will now find the real friend and the rhyme for *ball of twine,* and solve the rest of the riddles. *You* will have a restful vacation in the country—locked up in this house!" He chortled. "You'll be quite safe here! The cottage is totally isolated, so don't bother to yell for help. We've rented it for a month—but I do hope you won't have to stay that long!"

"Enough!" said Winifred. "Shall we escort the boys to their quarters?"

Cecil nodded and raised his walking stick as if to herd the boys with it. The Percivals closed in on The Three Investigators.

"Ramble and scramble," yelled Jupiter suddenly.

Bob and Pete responded instantly to their leader's signal. All three boys ran in different directions at once—darting toward and then veering away from windows, doors to other rooms, and even the Percivals themselves. Their captors tried to grab them, but it was like trying to stop a swarm of insects. The boys were everywhere at once—and suddenly they were gone! They escaped through the front door, back door, and a window, leaving the Percivals too confused to act for a moment.

Pete led the flight down the narrow road and onto the road back to town. The boys scanned the countryside as they ran, looking for a house or some shrubbery that they could take cover in. But the land was open and empty here. They had no choice but to keep running.

Tires squealed behind them. Bob flung a look back and gulped. The Percivals' car was just turning into the road to town!

"Jupe!" he gasped. "They're after us!"

"Go cross country," ordered Pete.

As one, the boys ran across the road, jumped the drainage ditch, and started to run across a field. There was another violent squeal of tires behind, followed by a crashing, banging sound. The boys looked back in dread, expecting to see the Percivals' car coming across the field after them. An entirely different sight greeted their eyes.

The Percivals had crashed into the ditch on their own side of the road! The car's windshield was shattered and one tire had blown out. Cecil Percival stumbled out of the wreckage and shook his walking stick after a blue car that was roaring down the road past the boys.

"Gosh, what happened?" asked Pete as he watched Cecil limp around his car to extricate Winifred.

Jupe's eyes were on the other car, which was quickly vanishing. "A hit-and-run case, apparently," he said slowly. "I guess that blue car passed the Percivals and cut back in too soon, forcing them off the road. You know, that car looked vaguely familiar. Did anyone see who was in it?"

"Two people, I think," answered Bob. "The driver seemed to be pretty big—a big man."

"The giant again!" exclaimed Pete.

"Perhaps," said Jupiter. "Or perhaps just a reckless driver speeding on the mountain roads."

"Well, whoever it was did us a real favor," said Pete.

"That's a switch!" said Bob. "People we don't know are usually trying to stop us!"

"Hey, look!" exclaimed Pete, pointing.

Winifred and Cecil were hobbling up the road toward their cottage. They looked back once at the boys, Cecil shaking his stick impotently. The Percivals were out of the action!

The Investigators laughed with relief and started walking rapidly back to town. Occasionally they glanced back just to make sure the Percivals weren't following them after all. But the fat man and his skinny sister seemed gone for good.

Jupiter kicked at pebbles on the road. "How could I have let that woman fool me!" he muttered. "I should have remembered what Roger Callow said—that the Percivals hadn't seen Dingo in ten years. They know next to nothing of his life here." Jupe hated to make a mistake—and he'd already made several bloopers on this case. He was humiliated.

"Well, gee, Jupe," Pete said consolingly, "she told us a pretty good story. And the cottage was right where we expected Dingo's friend to be. If you ask me, the Percivals were just lucky."

"And their luck's run out now!" said Jupe, cheering up. "Not only are they minus a car—and probably in hot water with some rental company—but they're going to have a hard time finding out who Dingo's friend really was!"

"How so?"

"Because the people most likely to know Dingo's friends are the Townes and Mr. Callow—and they'll never tell the Percivals!"

"But they'll tell us!" exclaimed Bob.

"Exactly," agreed Jupe. "Come on, let's go see the Townes! Look for a bus stop."

The road they were on soon turned onto a main road, and the boys spotted a bus stop not far away. But before a bus came, the mother of one of their classmates drove by in a station wagon. She stopped and offered the boys a lift.

The boys rode to Dingo's place and called at the Townes' cottage. Nelly Towne was there alone.

"I'm afraid Billy's sulking out in back, and Roger had

to drive to Los Angeles after he brought Billy home," she explained. "I'm just about to have lunch. Will you join me, and tell me the news?"

Over sandwiches, Bob told her what had happened. She was furious.

"Winifred and Cecil are too greedy. You mustn't trust them," she said.

"Don't worry!" exclaimed Pete. "Never again!"

"We think we have the answer to the last clue of the second riddle," said Jupe. "It means a *real* ride on a bus, to a *real* friend. Who would that friend be?"

Mrs. Towne thought. "Dingo's only good friends were Jack Dillon and Sadie Jingle. Sadie lives nearby, within walking distance, so it must be Jack. Dingo did take the bus to Dillon's once or twice a week. He caught the bus right out front."

"Dillon is the man who filed the will," Jupiter remembered. "It must be him! Where does he live, ma'am?"

"A mile or two past the county park, in a shack up a side road. You can't see it from the road, but he has a sign out you can see easily from the bus. The number eight bus."

They thanked her and hurried out to the bus stop across the street. As they reached the far curb, Jupiter stopped so suddenly that Bob nearly ran into him.

"Jupe, what—?" Bob protested.

Jupiter's eyes were shining. "Records! Second! I think I know what the bus clue means—and what to look for on the bus!"

11 ✦ The Tenth Ball of Twine

"Wow!" Pete cried. "What is it, Jupe?"

"Listen," he said as he took out his copy of the riddles. "Here's Riddle Three:

At the tenth ball of twine, you and me
see our handsome mug ahead."

He grinned. "What are there a lot of that you can always see from a bus, and that rhyme with *ball of twine?* Something Mrs. Towne just said we could see from the bus!"

"Gosh," Pete recalled, "she said we *couldn't* see Dillon's shack. I don't remember . . ."

"But we can see his sign!" Bob cried. "Signs!"

"Yes, signs," Jupiter said. "Old Dingo took the same bus, to the same friend, every week, and the next clue is the tenth *ball of twine* you can see from that bus! We don't need to see Jack Dillon, fellows. We just have to count ten signs on the bus route from Dingo's house to Dillon's!"

The boys waited with growing excitement. The number eight bus finally stopped in front of Dingo's place. As soon as the boys got on, they began to count the signs by the side of the road. The bus went along between the Botanical Gardens and the shopping center, turned up through the Gardens and the park, and continued on in the hills—fortunately into an area far from the Percivals' cottage.

As the boys counted the eighth sign, Bob shook his head unhappily. "Something's not right, Jupe," he said.

The eighth sign after Dingo's house was the sign for Jack Dillon's shack up the side road! The bus was stopping by it now.

"Yes," Jupiter agreed glumly.

"But," Pete wondered, "what's wrong, fellows? We haven't even reached the tenth sign yet."

"That's just it, Pete," Bob explained. "It doesn't seem right that Dingo would have meant a sign *past* where he got off!"

"Excuse me, boys."

Startled, the Investigators looked up. The bus driver stood in front of them. The boys had been so intent on their problem that they hadn't noticed the driver moving up the aisle from passenger to passenger.

"Another ten cents each, please," said the driver.

"Hunh?" said Pete.

"We're crossing into a higher fare zone," explained the driver. "If you want to keep riding, you have to pay another dime."

"Nuts!" said Pete as he started to rise. "We'll get off here!"

"Wait, Second!" ordered Jupe, pulling his companion back onto the seat. "We'd better keep riding to the tenth sign, just in case. Don't forget how tricky Dingo can be." He fished thirty cents out of his pocket and handed it to the driver.

The bus started up again and the tenth sign came—a

Do Not Enter sign on an exit from the freeway! Jupiter shook his head, and reached for the pull cord to signal that they wanted to get off at the next stop.

"Jupe!" Pete said. "Don't pull it!"

The Second Investigator pointed. A shiny new car was parked off the road near the freeway exit, and Winifred and Cecil Percival were standing in front of the Do Not Enter sign. The couple were arguing violently, and as the boys rode on past, they saw fat Cecil kick the sign and hop away holding his toe!

"Oh, no!" groaned Bob. "They're back in the game already!"

Pete grinned. "But they haven't found the right sign, either."

"No," Jupiter agreed, "but they've apparently figured out what *ball of twine* means. And they must have guessed that the *friend* was Jack Dillon—because his name was on the will as a witness! We'll ride to the next stop, but then we'll have to move fast."

At the next stop, out of sight of the Percivals, the boys got off. Pete watched the bus drive on and shrugged his shoulders unhappily.

"Well, what do we do now?" he asked.

"That," Jupiter said, "is no problem. The tenth sign out is past Dillon's shack and meaningless. So there can be only one answer. Old Dingo wrote *rides from a friend.* We wondered why he wrote *from,* remember? Now we know. He meant the tenth sign on the way *home* from Dillon's shack!"

"Of course," Bob said. "On the other side of the road. We'll get the next bus back!"

When the return bus came, they had to pay an extra

dime immediately because of being in the higher fare zone.

"What a rip-off!" complained Bob as he dug in his pocket for another coin. "We should have gone back to the depot and picked up our bikes."

"It's the price you pay for getting bus service this far out of town," lectured Jupe. "Now watch out for the Percivals—and the signs."

But when the bus went by the freeway exit, the Percivals were no longer around. The boys started watching for the sign to Dillon's shack, and began their count as soon as they passed it.

This time the eighth sign came well before they reached their final destination. The eighth was close to the main bus stop in the county park, and the ninth was a "slow" sign on the mountainside where the road curved down to the reservoir and dam.

"I bet it'll be a sign in the park or the Botanical Gardens!" Pete exclaimed.

"Yes," Jupiter agreed. "It looks to me like the whole search is to be around the park, all right."

As the bus continued downhill, they all leaned forward eagerly, waiting for the next sign. It came.

"Gosh," Pete said.

Bob grunted, "Oh."

"I . . . I . . . don't see—" Jupiter stammered.

The tenth sign back from Dillon's shack was a billboard where the county line ended and the city began:

WELCOME TO ROCKY BEACH

"Jupe, Dingo couldn't mean that sign," Bob said.

"No," Jupiter replied slowly. "We've made some mistake, fellows."

Pete suddenly exclaimed, "We're not the only ones who made a mistake! Look!"

A familiar red car was parked beside the road, and Skinny Norris was digging wildly in the dirt around the billboard! Judging by the number of holes in the ground, Skinny had been digging for some time. His face was red with frustration, and even as the bus sailed past, he flung his shovel away and glared at the sign.

"At least we know Skinny hasn't found anything," Bob said.

"Not yet," Jupiter said grimly, "but he's neck and neck with us, fellows. So are the Percivals. We've no time to waste."

"What do we do?" Bob asked. "What mistake did we make?"

"I don't know," Jupiter said. "But I'm sure we're up against one of Dingo's tricks. We'll have to go back to Riddle Two and complete the step we skipped—a visit to Jack Dillon!" Exasperated, he yanked on the stop cord.

Half an hour later the boys were walking up Jack Dillon's road. It ended at an unpainted, tumble-down shack with a wide dirt yard in front. As they crossed, Pete suddenly yelled:

"Get down!"

Like a big bird, the weird object sailed through the air straight toward their heads!

12·The Old Bushranger

It swooped down, gleaming in the sun like a miniature V-shaped spaceship!

It came down on top of them . . . and suddenly rose up, sailed on past them, curved in a wide arc, and vanished behind the shack!

"What . . . what was it?" Pete gasped.

A loud laugh came from behind the shack, and a small old man with stringy gray hair stepped out toward the boys. He wore a bush jacket, heavy trousers, and miner's boots. He carried the strange V-shaped object in his right hand.

"Scared the britches off you, did I?" He chuckled and waved the heavy wooden object at them. "Lay out a kangeroo at fifty yards, it will!"

Bob exclaimed, "A boomerang! It's a boomerang!"

"You could have hurt us!" Pete cried hotly.

"Cor," the small man said, his blue eyes twinkling, "not on your life. Jack Dillon can throw his boomer on a dime! Best thrower in Queensland in my time, bar none."

"Does it really always come back to you?" Bob asked.

"If you know how to throw it, young fellow," Dillon said.

"And if it misses the target," added Jupiter. "Origi-

nally, the purpose of the boomerang was to hit something—it's a special kind of throwing stick. The aborig-
ines in Australia used it for hunting and warfare."

"Aye, the fat lad's right. A smart one," Jack Dillon
said. His blue eyes darkened. "Now, what do you want
here?"

Bob and Pete started to explain who they were.

"I know who you are," Dillon interrupted. "You're
the scamps helping Nelly Towne and Callow find
Dingo's fortune. Why come to me? I don't know where
it is. Wouldn't tell if I did!"

Jupiter, who hated to be called fat, said stiffly, "We
think you do have the answer to one of the clues—even
if you don't know you do."

"Do you now? Well, if Dingo had wanted Nelly
Towne to have his swag he'd have left it to her straight
out. But he made the new will, told me to file it if he
died sudden, and—"

"You mean he *expected* to die suddenly?" Bob
exclaimed.

"I'm not saying what he expected. He had a bad heart
and was on all sorts of medicine. Living on borrowed
time, in fact. Not that we hadn't lived risky all our lives,
me and Dingo. Bushrangers together as lads, miners
and prospectors later, and I'll not help anyone to break
his last testament."

Jupiter said, "You think the will isn't a joke?"

"Dingo loved his jokes, and a good one it is." Dillon
chuckled. Then his eyes narrowed. "What else he might
have had in mind, I wouldn't be saying."

"Maybe you want the fortune for yourself!" Pete said

fiercely. "You must know rhyming slang better than anyone."

"Watch your tongue, boy!" Dillon snapped. "A pal's a pal, dead or alive. He took care of a pal with cash in the hand—I want none of his swag. Besides, I know the slang, but not all the rhymes in that will."

"You must know something important," Jupiter insisted. "About his regular visits to you. He—"

"I said I'll not help Nelly Towne!"

"Sir," Jupiter said quietly, "Dingo must have meant you to help everyone—one of the clues sent anyone who was searching to you. I'm certain Dingo intended his riddles to be fair. We're simply doing what he told us."

"Well . . . by golly, I suppose you're right! The foxy old rascal would want the game to be square—and he'd still beat you!" Dillon chuckled again. "I can almost hear him laughing, enjoying it wherever he is. All right, ask your questions."

"Well, sir," Jupiter began, "we've followed the riddles to you, and we know already that *ball of twine* means some road sign on the bus route back from here."

"Aye, that sounds logical. I didn't know *ball of twine* was rhymer-slang for a sign, but it fits. *You and me* is a cup of tea, *trouble and strife* is a wife, and *the old Ned*'s a bed. *Apples and pears* and *bottle and stopper* are real common. But I'm swoggled if I recognize any other rhymes in the riddles," Dillon said. His blue eyes twinkled wickedly. "O'course, old Dingo was fair fond of making up his own rhymes, and using ones he'd heard maybe once fifty years ago in some remote place in the Outback, so there's no way of being sure just what are rhymes and what aren't!" He laughed.

"Perhaps, sir," Jupiter said, looking annoyed. He disliked being laughed at almost as much as being called fat. "But we're quite sure that Dingo meant us to ride the same bus he rode between your house and his, and the tenth sign we saw would be a clue."

"Then why not do that and not bother me?"

"We did," Pete said unhappily, "but the tenth sign just can't be the clue—not coming or going."

"Now is that the truth?" Dillon said, and grinned. "Crafty old devil, wasn't he?"

"He was," Jupiter agreed, "so there has to be something special about Dingo's ride on the bus. Something I think only you would know, Mr. Dillon."

"Ah, you think that, do you? Now I wonder what that special thing could be?" The small man's eyes twinkled again.

"I think you know now, Mr. Dillon, don't you?" Jupiter said.

"By jingo, you are a smart lad," Dillon said, and nodded. "Yes, Dingo did ride the bus in a special way. If you knew him, you wouldn't have been surprised."

"What way, sir?" Bob demanded.

Dillon chuckled. "Dingo, my lads, was a man who took care of his money. It happens that on the bus going *into* town my stop is the last in a higher fare zone. So, to save ten cents, Dingo always walked down one stop before he got the bus!"

Pete found his voice first. "You mean, we have to count ten signs not from your stop but from the next stop!"

"Aye, I expect that's what the old rascal meant," Dillon said with his wicked grin.

They could still hear the old man laughing as they ran down the side road to the bus stop.

"We should have guessed it," Jupe said. "It was right here that the driver collected an extra dime on the way out. Drat!"

"And he'll collect an extra dime on the way in, too!" Pete pointed out. "We ought to walk down one stop, the way Dingo did."

"Good idea!" said Bob.

They saw only one sign as they walked from Dillon's road to the next bus stop.

"That means we want the first sign after the Welcome one," said Bob.

The bus came and again they counted signs as they rode. Down through the park they went. Skinny was no longer digging by the Welcome to Rocky Beach sign, they noted. They looked eagerly ahead as the bus passed the Botanical Gardens and the deputy's substation. But there were no more signs before the park road reached Dingo's street.

Then the bus turned onto Dingo's street . . . and a sign appeared down the block:

Turn left here for

FAIRVIEW SHOPPING MALL

"But," Pete wailed, "that's no better than the others! A whole shopping center!"

"I'm sure it's the right sign," said Jupe as he pulled

the stop cord. "Somewhere in there we'll have to find the next clue."

The boys hopped off the bus and walked across the street to the shopping center. It was a vast place, with a giant supermarket, restaurants and taverns, and rows of small shops. Slowly the Investigators looked around and groaned.

13 ✦ Danger Ahead!

"It's got to be another wrong sign," Bob said glumly as he surveyed the shopping center.

"If it isn't," Pete said, "this is the end of one swell treasure hunt."

"Maybe we miscounted," Bob suggested hopefully, "or overlooked some small sign between the ninth and this one."

"Sure!" Pete exclaimed. "Some really small sign!"

"No," Jupiter said. "I'm convinced that the Shopping Mall sign is the correct one this time. We discovered Dingo's special bus habits and we counted carefully, so the next clue must be here."

"Where?" Bob sighed, looking at all the stores.

"We've followed all the riddles correctly so far," Jupiter said. "There's a definite pattern emerging. When one clue sends us to a place, the next clue tells us what to look for when we get there."

The stocky leader took out his page of riddles. "The *friend* sent us to the *ball of twine*—actually to the shopping mall. So, the next clue in Riddle Three has to tell us what to look for here."

He read the third riddle aloud:

> "*At the tenth ball of twine, you and me
> see our handsome mug ahead.*"

Bob said, "And *you and me* is rhyming slang for a cup of tea."

"Swell," Pete muttered, looking around the vast area jammed with shoppers. "Anyone see a nice cup of tea waiting for us?"

"No," Jupiter said, "but I see where we could get one!" He pointed in triumph. "Look over there!"

Bob and Pete looked. Between a cheese shop and a rug store was The Stratford Tea Shoppe! A sign with Old English lettering hung from its half-timbered facade, and small cakes were displayed behind its leaded windows.

"A little restaurant," Bob said.

"Yes," Jupiter said, "and we're only a few blocks from old Dingo's house here. I'll bet he used to come here for tea."

They walked over to the Tea Shoppe and went inside. The restaurant had a series of small rooms with low ceilings, just like a real tea shop in England. Mounted fish and animal heads and framed photographs of Rocky Beach scenes decorated the walls. The small tables were crowded with shoppers having tea and cakes and other snacks. A pretty hostess came up to the Investigators.

"Can I help you, boys?"

Jupiter's voice was dignified. "Did Mr. Marcus Towne frequent this establishment, miss?"

"Yes, he did. At least three or four times a week."

"Of course," Jupiter went on wisely, "he had his own private mug. May we please see it?"

"Mug?" The hostess was puzzled. "He had no mug."

"Then he must have liked one of yours. Could we—"

"We don't use any mugs. We use cups."

"N–no mugs?" Jupiter said. "Then . . . then . . ."

Deflated, Jupiter couldn't even finish his sentence. He'd been so sure!

"Maybe," Bob put in, "you could tell us what he did here, miss? I mean, anything he did regularly?"

"Did? Why, he came in the late afternoon—just about this time—had two or three cups of Oolong and a soft roll, and left."

"Oolong?" Pete repeated.

"It's a Chinese tea," the hostess explained. "Our best. We serve a great deal of it."

Bob pondered. "Did Mr. Towne sit at a special table, miss?"

"Well, he usually asked for table six, and sat there if it wasn't already taken."

Jupiter revived. "That must be it! May we see the table?"

"Well, I suppose so. It's empty at the moment."

They followed the hostess to a table in a corner. A giant swordfish was mounted above it on the wall. Pete sat down and his face fell.

"Gosh, all you can see from here is the opposite wall!"

Bob sat down, too. "Just the wall ahead, Jupe. All that's on it is a deer head, a big mirror, and a couple of photographs. There's no mug."

"Jupe," Pete exclaimed, "the deer head has a nose! That's the next clue, isn't it?"

Jupiter read Riddle Four:

"One man's victim is another's darlin',
follow the nose to the place.

"A stuffed deer is certainly a *victim*," he went on, "and *deer* sounds like *dear,* which is the same as *darling!*"

"But," Bob said, "the nose of the deer doesn't point at anything except this table!"

Jupiter nodded glumly. "Maybe those photographs?"

They crossed the room and looked closely at the photos on the wall. One was of an old Rocky Beach hotel torn down years ago, and the other was of a past Fiesta Day parade. Jupiter shook his head.

"Maybe something's hidden around the table," Bob ventured.

They searched around and under Dingo's table but found nothing. The hostess looked at her watch.

"We're very busy, boys. You'll have to leave now if you don't wish to order."

Crushed, the Investigators left the tea shop. It was getting late, almost time for dinner.

"I'm starved," Pete said. "Let's give up and go get our bikes so we can go home."

"Yes," Jupiter agreed sadly. "But first, let's go see Mrs. Towne. The tea shop might mean more to her than to us."

They walked the few blocks to the white cottage. Mrs. Towne was still alone. She stood at a window and barely listened to the boys' description of the tea shop.

"I don't know anything about that tea shop, boys."

"Maybe Oolong means something special," Bob said.

"What?" Mrs. Towne said, distracted. "I'm sorry, boys. I'm watching for Billy. He hasn't been home since lunch. Oolong? It's just a tea Dingo liked, and . . . Thank goodness, there's Billy now, and with Roger!"

She hurried to the door to let Billy and Roger Callow in. Billy looked defiant.

"I spotted him at the shopping mall on my way home," Callow said.

Pete exclaimed, "He must have been following us again!"

"You don't own the streets!" Billy cried. "I wasn't—"

"Hush now, Billy!" said Mrs. Towne. "You know what I said about running off on your own."

Roger Callow said, "Well, never mind now. Fill me in on what you've learned, boys. I've been away all day."

The lawyer paced the cottage as the boys told him what had happened since they'd seen him near the bus depot that morning.

"You're sure there was no mug at the tearoom?" Callow said.

"We're sure," Jupiter said. "Perhaps Dingo had one in his house?"

Roger Callow hurried across the yard to the tumble-down house. Everyone followed him inside and searched the dusty rooms. The only mug they found was a plain brown one, with no markings.

"This can't be the right mug," said Jupiter. "There's nothing on it that points us to the next clue. This is hopeless."

"It certainly is," said Roger Callow. Exasperated, he

hurled the mug on the floor, smashing it. He flushed.

"I'm sorry, boys, but I'm worried. We must find the gems! The Percivals or that Norris boy could easily beat us!"

Billy said, "Mom, Granddad used to—"

"It's your bath time, young man. Off with you, now!"

The small boy stormed off toward the cottage.

Roger Callow paced the dusty old house. "Is there a rhyme for mug?"

"Nothing we saw in the tea shop," Jupiter said. "Not too much rhymes with mug—*bug, hug, lug, rug*—"

"Well, you had better find an answer soon," the lawyer said sharply, "or I'll have to hire a real agency after all!"

Dejected, the boys left Dingo's house in silence and walked out to the street to catch a bus back to the depot. As they approached the bus stop, Bob started.

"Hey, fellows, there's that car again!"

A familiar blue car was parked across the street—and a giant man lurked behind it in the shadows of the trees!

"That's three times now, at least!" exclaimed Jupiter softly. "It can't be coincidence anymore. He must be watching us or—"

"Jupe!" Pete whispered, "there's another man, too!"

A smaller shadow had joined the giant.

"Let's try to hear what they say," Jupiter urged. "Pretend we're walking home, then cut back!"

The boys walked up the hill beyond Dingo's property, over the crest and out of sight of the shadowy watchers. Then they darted across the street and deep into the trees. Stealthily they crept back toward the two men.

When they knew they were close, Pete raised his head.

"The big one's alone again!" he whispered.

A twig broke behind them! The boys whirled. A thin man with fierce eyes stood there. His hat brim was pulled low, and his black suit jacket hung open to reveal a pistol in a holster! His voice was sharp with menace:

"What are you kids doing?"

The giant appeared on the other side! A massive six-foot-nine, he had a flat nose, cauliflower ears, and enormous arms.

Pete blurted, "Why are you watching us!"

"Who says we're watching you?" the giant growled.

"Then what are you doing?" Bob demanded.

"Minding our own business, kid," the smaller man said. "You better do the same. Now get lost—fast!"

Gulping, the boys ran out of the trees and up the hill as fast as they could. Flinging a look back, they saw a bus approaching and raced to meet it at the next stop. Not until the bus had taken them halfway into town did they feel safe enough to relax.

"Who do you think those men are?" Bob finally asked.

"I don't know, but the smaller one had a gun," said Jupe. "Detectives, perhaps, or thugs! Crooks after the gems! Maybe someone hired them."

"The Percivals?" Bob said.

"Possibly," Jupiter replied. "Fellows, we *must* find out what *see our handsome mug ahead* means!"

Pete groaned. "With those thugs around, all I see ahead is danger!"

14 · Pete Finds the Handsome Mug

Pete took a bite of his fifth waffle. It was Sunday-brunch time at the Crenshaws'. Mr. and Mrs. Crenshaw were absorbed in the newspaper. Pete was meditating on The Three Investigators' latest problem—the elusive handsome mug.

The investigation seemed to be stalled. The boys had all had to stay home the night before, and morning phone calls to each other before church had produced no new ideas about the unsolved clue.

"Dad, what could a mug be besides a mug?"

"What?" Mr. Crenshaw lowered his paper. "A mug is a mug." He raised his paper again. "Unless it's a second-rate man."

"I don't see how that helps," Pete muttered.

Mr. Crenshaw paused in his reading. "You're sure you're not thinking of a mugger? A person who hits you and robs you?"

"No, it's mug, all right," Pete said, sighing.

"Well," Mr. Crenshaw said from behind the paper, "how about mug shots? You know—police photos, close-ups of crooks' faces."

"Mug shots?" Pete said. His eyes widened. "That's it!"

"What?" Mr. Crenshaw said from behind the newspaper.

But Pete was already dialing Headquarters. There was no answer. He dialed Jupiter's home number. Jupiter came to the phone.

"May-day!" Pete cried. "I've got it. Call Bob!"

He hung up and rushed out to his bike. Minutes later he crawled up into the hidden trailer. Jupiter was there, but not Bob.

"Bob's on the way," Jupiter said. "What have you got, Second?"

"The answer to *see our handsome mug ahead!*" Pete said. He grinned and sat down. "I'm looking at it now!"

Jupiter blinked and looked around. "Where?"

Before Pete could answer, the telephone rang. Jupiter picked it up. Mrs. Towne was calling.

"Billy's vanished again, Jupiter," the agitated mother said. "He said something this morning about knowing what *mug* meant. I think he went off to that tea shop. He's been gone a long time and I'm worried. Some strange-looking men have been hanging around, and I think I saw the Percivals' car near here earlier."

"Is one of the strange men almost a giant?"

"Yes, the same man we saw before! I called Roger, but he wasn't home."

"We'll go to the tea shop at once," Jupiter promised. "Did Billy say what he thought *mug* meant?"

"No," Mrs. Towne replied. "Please hurry, Jupiter."

Jupiter said they would. As he hung up, Bob crawled up into the trailer. Jupiter reported what Mrs. Towne had said, adding grimly, "If something happened to Billy, the Percivals would be next in line for Dingo's fortune!"

"But what's Pete's answer to the riddle?" Bob asked.

"I'm looking at it." Pete grinned from his chair.

"Where?" Bob stared all around just as Jupiter had.

"Right in front of both of you!"

Jupiter scowled. "This is no time for jokes, Second."

"All I see," Bob said, "is the desk, the wall, Jupe's old mirror, the bust of Shakespeare, the—"

"Oh!" Jupiter cried, his face turning beet red. He hated to be outguessed. "*Our* handsome mug! Another Dingo trick!"

"Where?" Bob said again, annoyed. "What are you talking about?"

"The mirror, Bob!" Jupiter said. "We can see—our *faces!* Mug is slang for face. There's a mirror on the tea shop wall facing table six. *See our handsome mug ahead* means look in that mirror!"

"So let's go and see what it shows!" Pete said.

They crawled out, got their bikes, and rode to Dingo's favorite tea shop. It was open but few people were in it before noon. Billy wasn't there. The same hostess was.

"Yes, there was a small boy here about an hour ago," the hostess said. "He sat at table six, then went out."

"Was anyone else around, miss?" Jupiter asked.

"A fat man and a thin woman came in just before the boy. They asked about Mr. Towne, and I mentioned table six. They sat down, but they didn't seem pleased as the boy did."

"Thank you, miss," said Jupiter, and turned to his companions.

"The Percivals," Bob said. "You think they grabbed Billy?"

"Or perhaps followed him," Jupiter said.

"How do we find him now?" Pete wondered.

"He must have discovered the answer to the *mug* riddle, Pete, and if he left here looking pleased, I'll bet he figured out the next clue," Jupiter said. "To find him, we'll have to figure it out, too!"

At table six, Jupiter sat down and looked into the mirror across the room. Bob and Pete peered over his shoulder.

"Well," Jupiter said, "I see myself, the table, the swordfish mounted on the wall above the table, an old menu on the wall, two more photographs, and . . . and that's all."

"Read the next riddle, Jupe," Bob suggested.

Jupiter read it:

> *"One man's victim is another's darlin',*
> *follow the nose to the place."*

Bob said, "Dingo couldn't mean any particular face in the mirror. He wouldn't know who'd be looking."

Pete said, "The photos are both of the harbor—no *victim* or *darling* there—and I don't see any noses but ours."

"How about the old menu?" Bob said.

"No," Jupiter said slowly. He was pinching his lower lip, as he always did when he was thinking hard. "I believe I understand the clue, but I have to be sure. Come on."

The stocky leader of the trio went to the hostess and asked for the public telephone.

"We don't have one. Try the gas station across the mall."

The station was closed, but there was a phone booth outside. Jupiter dialed Jack Dillon's number.

"You again," the peppery old man said.

"Sir," Jupiter said, "you told us yesterday that you didn't recognize all of the rhyming slang in Dingo's riddles. But might you recognize a rhyme if I told you it was a *reverse* rhyme?"

"Reverse, my brainy rascal? Just how do you mean?"

"I think that Dingo has used a word for which there is a slang rhyme, and he wants us to discover what the slang term is. I mean, instead of using the rhyming slang, he's given us what the slang *means,* and we have to work backwards. Riddle Four starts out, *one man's victim is another's darlin'.* Is there a slang rhyme that *means* darling? Maybe—something *marlin?*"

"So," Dillon chortled, "you've figured that out, too?"

"Too?" Jupiter said quickly. "Someone else called you?"

"Young Billy Towne, not an hour ago," Dillon said. "Dingo's a sly old snake, eh? Yes, lad, down under a man's darlin' is called his *briny marlin,* right enough."

Jupiter thanked the old man, hung up, and started back to the tea shop. Pete and Bob hurried along with him.

"But," Pete said, puzzled, "what does *marlin* mean, Jupe?"

"A marlin," Jupiter announced, "is a large fish—a kind of swordfish! That fish on the wall is actually a marlin!"

"Wow," Pete exclaimed, "and does it ever have a nose!"

Back in the tea shop, the hostess looked a little annoyed as the boys hurried to the big marlin mounted over table six. Bob sighted along the sword.

"It points straight at a photograph up front!"

They went to the framed photo on the front wall, squeezed in between the corner and a display window.

"Why," Pete declared, "it's a shot of Rocky Beach Town Hall! It's old, but the town hall's still the same."

"So *follow the nose to the place* means," Jupiter said, "go where the marlin's nose points—to the town hall!"

"Where," Bob realized, "men *buy* their *trouble and strife!* The Marriage License Bureau! That's why Dingo said *buy!*"

"I'm certain of it," Jupiter agreed. "Billy must be there already. We'd better call Mrs. Towne and tell her."

They went back to the closed gas station and Jupiter started to call Mrs. Towne. Pete suddenly came alert.

"Jupe! Bob! Listen!" the tall boy said.

Jupiter stopped dialing. They all heard it—a strange, dragging sound like something heavy rasping over metal!

"What is—?" Pete said.

"It's inside the gas station!" Bob said.

They stared at the closed and silent gas station. Then they heard another sound—a distant, muffled voice:

"Help! Help!"

15·Get Out if You Can!

They peered inside the locked gas station.

"I don't see anyone!" Pete declared.

"Help! Help!!" The call was still faint.

Bob cried, "It's coming from behind the station!"

Behind the empty station they saw three parked cars and a closed van. The heavy, dragging sound came again.

"In the van," Pete said.

"Help!" the muffled voice called again.

"It's Billy!" Jupiter exclaimed. "Open the van!"

The van doors weren't locked, and when the boys pulled them open, they saw a big pile of ground cloths used by mechanics when they worked under cars. The pile moved and hit a heavy pulley that was dangling from the roof of the van, making it rasp and drag against the metal sides!

The boys pulled at the mound of ground cloths until they uncovered the small boy. He was tied hand and foot, with a bag over his head! As they freed him, he struggled up, pale but still eager and defiant.

"What happened, Billy?" asked Bob.

"I remembered that Granddad always said that people had ugly mugs or handsome mugs, so I figured out the mirror clue," Billy said proudly. "I saw the big fish, knew it was a marlin, and saw that its sword pointed to the town hall picture. I called Mr. Dillon to be sure. When I hung up, you fellows called to me from behind the gas station—I mean, whoever it was said he was Pete. When I came back, he dropped the bag over my head and grabbed me! I never saw who it was, and the next thing I knew I was under those cloths. I started kicking and yelling!"

"That was good thinking," Pete said.

"I saw the Percivals and that Skinny Norris hanging around earlier," Billy admitted. "I guess I talked too loud on the phone and gave away what I knew. Goofed again!" He looked dejected.

"You did very well to work out the riddle by yourself," Jupiter said approvingly, "and you were brave not to panic. We all make mistakes. You'll be more careful in the future."

"Then can I work with you guys now?" begged Billy. "Can I? Please? I promise I'll be real careful and do just what you say."

"Well . . ." Jupe stalled.

"Why not?" said Pete. "The kid's just proved he can take the pressure—and he solved one clue faster than we did! Let him come along, Jupe."

"Okay by me," put in Bob.

"All right," said Jupe at last. "You can work with us from now on, Billy—*if* your mother agrees."

Mrs. Towne was relieved when Jupiter reported Billy safe, but she hesitated when Jupiter asked her to let Billy join them.

"He's a smart boy," Jupiter said, "and, besides, I think it's more dangerous to have him running around on his own, ma'am."

"Perhaps you're right," Mrs. Towne agreed. "Very well, but keep a sharp eye on him, Jupiter Jones."

Jupiter reported the good news to Billy and they retrieved his bike where it was parked near the tea shop. Now a quartet, they rode through the quiet Sunday streets into downtown Rocky Beach. A few people were wandering around the courthouse and town hall. Although closed for business on Sundays, the beautiful buildings remained open as tourist attractions.

The Marriage License Bureau was a small, first-floor room at the left rear corner of the town hall. The boys went into the empty room, and Jupiter read out the fifth riddle:

> *"Where men buy their trouble and strife,*
> *get out if you can."*

They looked around the small, quiet room. The closed business windows were on the right, in front of the rear wall of the town hall. To their left a tall writing counter ran the length of the wall. Ahead was a long, high-backed wooden bench under two barred windows. Official announcements and portraits of the governor and the mayor hung on the walls.

"Okay," Pete said, "here's where men buy a wife—I mean, a marriage license. Now what is *get out if you can* a rhyme for in the room?"

"Or a reverse rhyme," Bob said. "Or maybe it's one of those no-rhyme clues."

Jupiter pondered. "Remember that whatever *get out if*

you can is, it has to lead us to the next clue—which is the first clue in the sixth and last riddle:

In the posh Queen's old Ned, be bright
and natural, and the prize is yours.

"Something in this room should point us to a queen or a bed."

"Gosh," Billy said, "I don't see anything that looks like a queen, or a bed, or that's even very bright."

"No," Jupiter said slowly. "But the *posh Queen's old Ned* won't necessarily be in this room. Let's try a reverse rhyme in Riddle Five. For a reverse rhyme to work, one of the words in the clue has to be a single thing—like a darling, or a copper, or a pistol. If we think of *get out* as meaning *escape* it could work."

"Maybe a fire escape!" Billy suggested.

But the room was on the first floor. There was no fire escape anywhere near it.

"That wouldn't be a rhyme anyway," Bob objected. "Just the same word."

"A window?" Pete wondered. "They're barred, so they're hard to get out through."

"Window isn't a rhyme for *get out* or *escape* either," Bob said. "Not much is."

They looked out the windows anyway, and saw nothing but the bushes growing outside. The view out the door provided no clue to a queen or a bed either.

"Let's try to find a rhyme for *can* then," Jupiter said.

"Ban, fan, man, pan, ran, tan," recited Bob.

"Hey, the walls are tan!" said Billy.

"True," said Jupiter, "but that doesn't help us solve the clue. There's also a man here—two men, in fact, in the photographs of the mayor and the governor. But I can't see how they'd fit in with the clue."

"How about a ban on something in one of the announcements on the wall?" asked Bob.

The boys rushed to read the various documents, which mostly related to the requirements for getting a marriage license. They found several rules forbidding something, but none seemed to fit the clue.

Jupiter finally announced, "I don't think *get out if you can* is a rhyming clue at all."

"It's another of Dingo's tricks!" Pete moaned.

"Perhaps it's simply a literal instruction to find a way out of here," said Jupe.

"How?" asked Bob. "The windows are barred, there's no fire escape nearby, and there's only one door—the door we came in."

"Fellows!" Jupiter suddenly pointed to the floor near the door. "Look how the floor tiles are worn down where people walked in and out!"

Bob shrugged. "What about it, Jupe? That's normal."

"But look at the floor where the bench is!"

They all saw it—an identical path of worn floor tiles that stopped dead at the far wall!

"A secret door!" Bob and Pete cried together.

The boys ran to the wall and began to search. But the wall was just smooth, painted plaster with no cracks. Slowly, their excitement faded.

"A blank wall," Billy wailed. "That's all it is!"

Pete looked closely and said, "But there *was* a door

here. It's been walled up. Look, the paint here above the worn tiles is slightly lighter in color. Must have been put on in the last couple of months. But of course, it wasn't hard to get out this way when the door was here."

"A walled-up door," mused Jupiter. He blinked at the others and suddenly cried, "What street is out there, fellows? The street that exit would have gone to?"

"Street?" Bob puzzled. "Why Salsipuedes Street, I think. Yeah, that's right, but—"

Jupiter was already running out the door!

16 + Another Riddle Solved

Jupiter pounded out the front door of the town hall and around the building, with Bob, Pete, and Billy close behind him. Breathing hard, but with his eyes alight, Jupiter stopped along the side of the building where a recessed archway showed the former exit from the Marriage License Bureau.

"What are we doing, Jupe?" Pete panted.

"This way isn't *get out if you can*," Bob protested. "It's *get out if you can't!*"

"Yes," Jupiter puffed, "but Pete is right about a recently walled-up door. The brick in the old doorway is brand new! A few months ago we could have come out this way—and I'm certain that the last time old Dingo saw the town hall this door was still open!"

"But," Billy hesitated, "how does that fit the clue, Jupiter? I mean, if the door was still open, it'd be easy to get out."

"Sure," Pete agreed. "Billy's right, First."

"Yes," Jupiter said, his eyes gleaming, "but what does *Salsipuedes* mean, fellows? The name of the street this door used to lead to—what does it mean?"

"Mean?" Bob said slowly, and his eyes widened. "It's Spanish for *get out if you can!* Dingo meant—"

"For us to go out the Salsipuedes Street exit and look for the *posh Queen's old Ned!*" Jupiter finished.

The former exit had been at the side of the town hall, near the back. Thick bushes and trees grew close to the building, and a narrow pathway led out through them and across a lawn to Salsipuedes Street. The boys looked carefully around the bricked-up doorway for a solution to the next clue. Finding nothing, they hurried along the path toward the street.

As they came out into the open in the early afternoon sun, they all stopped. The Chamber of Commerce storefront office was directly across Salsipuedes Street— and in the display window was a large sign:

SEE A LEGEND OF THE SEA!!
S.S. Queen of the South
Fully Restored to
Its Original Glory
NOW OPEN
Souvenirs   Refreshments
Rocky Beach Harbor Wharf

"The Queen!" Pete cried. "The new tourist attraction!"

"Are you sure?" Billy said.

"Yes!" said Jupiter. "It's certainly a posh Queen, and on an ocean liner there are beds!"

"So the next step is to go to the Queen!" Pete said.

"And find the *old Ned!*" Bob added.

"We've almost got Granddad's fortune!" Billy crowed.

Jupiter only beamed, and started for the parking lot on the other side of the town hall, where they had left their bikes. Suddenly he stopped.

Someone was running away among the bushes! As the boys watched, the running figure emerged on the lawn halfway to the parking lot. Skinny Norris!

"After him!" Pete yelled. "He must have heard us!"

"The rotten sneak!" Bob cried as they pursued their old adversary. "He never could figure things out himself!"

They pounded up to the parking lot just in time to see Skinny's car back out and come roaring straight toward them. They jumped for safety. As Skinny drove by he thumbed his nose at them and laughed.

"Quick!" Jupiter urged. "The bikes!"

"But . . . but," Billy wailed, "we'll never catch him on bikes! He'll find the jewels first!"

"He still has to find the right bed," Jupiter said grimly, "and the right clue in the bed. Hurry, fellows!"

"Hey, the bikes are gone!" Pete cried.

Stunned, they looked around the parking lot.

"Skinny must have taken them and hidden them!" Bob said.

"Wait!" Jupiter said. "There they are!"

The four bikes were far across the parking lot, stashed in some shrubs between the lot and the side street. As the boys ran to get them, Billy tripped on a loose shoelace and bent down to tie it. The Investigators reached the bikes and turned to yell impatiently at the small boy.

"Hey, Billy!" Pete called. "Get a move—"

Before he could finish his sentence, two men appeared on top of the Investigators. The giant man, and

his smaller partner with the pistol under his jacket!
Without a word, the giant grabbed Pete and Jupiter and
the smaller man grabbed Bob. Helpless in their iron
grips, the three boys were hustled from the parking lot
and into a car!

17 ⋅ **Caught!**

"Be nice, kids, and you won't get hurt," the smaller man said from the driver's seat of the car.

The three boys were squeezed into the back seat, with Pete on one side of the giant and Bob and Jupiter on the other. Shades had been drawn over the rear windows!

"What about the other kid, Mr. Savo?" the giant asked.

"The party said we hold these three," the smaller man said. "Keep them quiet, Turk, and don't think. Okay?"

"Sure, boss," Turk said agreeably.

Scared by the pair of thugs, the boys rode in silence. Mr. Savo drove carefully, never speeding, and making many turns through the back streets of Rocky Beach. Slowly, the boys began to relax. Savo and Turk didn't seem to want to hurt them. Jupiter was the first to find his voice.

"Hold us for what?" the stout leader asked shakily.

Savo laughed in the front seat. "For a while, kid."

"No, I mean *who* are you holding us for?" Jupiter went on.

"I know what you meant," Savo snapped. "Just say we're doing a favor for a friend, okay?"

The giant Turk said, "You was in the way now."

"Shut up, Turk!" Savo said.

The smaller man, obviously the leader of the pair,

drove on in silence for a few more blocks. Then the car turned into a driveway on the west side of Rocky Beach and pulled up at a small cottage hidden behind a larger house.

"Out," Mr. Savo said.

Turk marched the boys inside the cottage, into a small rear room. There were three cots in the room. The door was covered with sheet metal and the one window was heavily shuttered. A second door led into a tiny, windowless bathroom.

"Okay," Mr. Savo said, "now—"

Jupiter interrupted, "What friend are you holding us for? Whoever it is, Mrs. Towne will pay you much more when we find—"

"Just someone wants you out of the way awhile, okay?"

"Why do it for him?" Bob exclaimed. "It's kidnaping!"

"Hey," Turk growled, "who you calling kidnapers?"

Mr. Savo scowled. "We're no kidnapers, punk!"

"Technically," Jupiter began, "you are—"

"Nuts!" Mr. Savo snarled, then shrugged. "Look, kids, we got nothing against you, see? We're only protecting our interest."

"What interest?" Pete said.

"Money, kid—what else? The party owes us money. Too much money for too long. We don't like that."

Turk laughed, shaking like a great, shaggy bear. "People that don't know how to play cards shouldn't oughta play, right, boss?"

"Shut up, Turk!" Mr. Savo said.

Bob gaped. "You're . . . you're gamblers!"

"Not gamblers, kid," Savo said. "The losers, they're gamblers. We're businessmen. People want to gamble, we give them a place and a time for it, but we don't gamble."

"Mr. Savo," Jupiter said, "whoever your friend is, I know Mrs. Towne will pay you more to let us go when we find her father-in-law's fortune. Or my uncle will pay—"

"I said we wasn't kidnapers, kid!" Savo said. "Just a straight business deal. We want what we're owed from the party in question, and nothing more. Nothing from you! Now you all shut up. You ask too many questions. Turk!"

The giant turned for the door. "You kids just be good."

"You've got beds and a toilet. There's food in that cabinet, and jugs of water. Just like home. Take a nice rest for a while. You can't get out of here."

With a nod, the smaller man led the giant out and the door closed. The boys heard the key turn in the lock and a heavy bar fall into place across the door. They were imprisoned!

Then the front door closed, but no car started. And someone was still in the outer room. They heard a chair creak heavily, then a deep, bearlike sigh.

"That Turk's still out there," Pete whispered.

Jupiter said softly, "First let's see if we can find any way out, then we'll worry about Turk."

Pete tiptoed to the door, Bob quietly examined all the windows, and Jupiter inspected the windowless bathroom. Pete was the first to admit defeat.

"The door's double-locked, covered with sheet metal so we can't take out any panels, and the hinges are outside," he reported, his voice low. "We've got nothing that could cut through the sheet metal, even if Turk wasn't out there."

Jupiter came out of the bathroom. "It's absolutely solid—not even a proper vent."

"The shutters are hopeless, too," Bob said. "They're bolted and hinged outside, and the slats are too heavy to break through."

"There's still the floor," Pete said.

They examined the floor. It didn't take long.

"The whole house is on a concrete slab," Pete announced, "and there are no heaters, or ducts, or vents, or anything in the walls." He sighed. "There's no way out of here, Jupe. We might as well lie down." And he did.

"Savo and Turk aren't amateurs," Jupiter said, his round face drooping. "I guess they know how to lock people in."

"Well," Bob said, taking the cot next to Pete, "that's the real end of a fine treasure hunt. Whoever told Savo and Turk to hold us must be on the *Queen of the South* right now!"

"Why didn't we bring our walkie-talkies or our direction-finders with us today?" moaned Jupiter.

"What good would that do?" answered Bob. "We're all in here together."

"We might have given one of them to Billy," said Jupe.

"Billy!" exclaimed Pete. "Maybe he saw us get

grabbed and called the cops!"

"Maybe they're looking for us right now!" added Bob.

"Don't count on it," warned Jupiter. "Billy wasn't even looking at us when we were caught. And if he did see us, he was too far away to read the license plate. He could only report that the getaway car was blue—and there must be a thousand blue cars in Rocky Beach!" The stocky boy sat down wearily on a cot.

"Maybe Billy went on down to the ship and is working on the next clue," suggested Bob. "He's a smart kid. Maybe he'll find the *old Ned.*"

"And maybe he'll find trouble!" Jupiter pointed out. "He'd be alone and exposed to danger! The Percivals could show up—and they might lose all scruples so close to the end of the hunt."

"Then good-bye, Billy!" commented Pete grimly.

Jupiter lay back on his cot with a sigh. There was nothing he could do to help the little boy—except pray that Billy kept his wits about him.

Hours passed. The boys watched the rays of sun through the shutter slats grow longer and longer. Once they heard Savo return, talk for a time with Turk, and then go away again. Pete finally got hungry and began to devour the food in the cabinet. The others nibbled at some bread and cheese to keep their strength up, but they had no appetite.

Jupiter lay on his cot, pinching his lower lip and thinking hard.

"Something is very strange," he said finally.

"What?" asked Pete.

"How did Turk and Savo get on to us in the first place? Why did they spy on us for days, without trying to stop us? I think they even tried to help us once, when they ran the Percivals off the road. It seems as if they were just waiting for us to lead them—or someone—to the gems. How did they know when to step in? Who told them to? Who wants the treasure—and wants us out of the way?"

"Gee, I don't know," said Pete. "The Percivals?"

"Perhaps, but I don't think they've been here long enough to run up gambling debts."

"It's probably someone we never heard of," said Bob.

"Maybe," said Jupe, and kept thinking.

The sunbeams through the shutters finally disappeared. The light in the locked room faded. They had been prisoners the whole afternoon! In the other room Turk began to snore. This time they were really defeated! They had solved the riddles right up to the last one—now someone else would finish the hunt. Someone who had tricked them!

On their cots in the dim silence, even they began to doze. What else was there to do? . . .

Pete sat up! "What was that?"

They listened. Turk's snores almost shook the house —but there was something else. A tapping!

"It's at the window!" Bob whispered.

A light tapping came from outside the window of the locked room, and a faint whispering: "Fellows? Jupiter? Pete?"

"In here, yes," Pete whispered back at the window. The window creaked, and they could hear heavy breathing as someone struggled to push the bolt back. Then it gave, and the shutters swung open. The boys gaped.

"Billy!" they all said together, almost too loud.

"Shhhh," the little boy said, grinning. "That big guy's asleep in a chair and I've got the front door blocked, but he could wake up any minute. Hurry!"

They needed no telling. Turk's rasping snores urged them out of the window fast enough. In the dusk, they hurried quietly around the house toward the street.

"But how did you find us, Billy?" Jupiter demanded.

"Well," the boy said happily as they reached the street, "when I saw them grab you, I tried to call Mr. Callow, but he wasn't home or at his office. I didn't want to scare my mom or your folks, but I was going to call Mr. Jones—when I got the idea."

"What idea?" Jupiter panted as they trotted on.

"A Ghost-to-Ghost Hookup!"

Pete almost stopped dead. "You used our Ghost-to—?"

"I heard about it before I met you, and I did it just the way you do. Except I used a phone booth for my headquarters. Some kid finally spotted the car."

"What a miracle!" exclaimed Pete. "You didn't even have the license number."

"Yes, I did!" said Billy proudly. "Those guys hung around my street so much that I finally got suspicious. I wrote down their license this morning. Just like a real de—"

There was a loud roar and a violent crash behind them!

"He's out, the big guy!" Billy cried. "I had garbage cans in front of the door! Run!"

They ran faster—down to the block to the avenue, around the corner, and wildly on.

"Hurry!" Bob puffed. "He's got the car!"

"No, he hasn't," Billy gasped, and held up a round black object. "I took the distributor cap out."

They all stopped running. Bob, Pete, and Jupiter began to laugh like maniacs. They could picture the giant Turk roaring with rage as he kept trying to start the car and nothing happened. Passersby stared, but the boys didn't care.

"A fine job, Billy. Congratulations," Jupiter announced between guffaws. Then he calmed down. "Only—I hope it's not too late!"

Everyone else stopped laughing.

"We won't know until we solve the last clue," Jupiter said. "Come on. We'll get our bikes and find *the Queen's old Ned!*"

18 ✦ A Near Miss

The bikes were still at the town hall. The four boys rode as fast as they could to the harbor. In a far corner of the harbor, the giant ocean liner soared up from the wharf. A few lights on it shone in the twilight. As the boys rode up, crowds of people streamed away from the ship along the wharf.

"Watch for Skinny and the Percivals!" Jupiter said.

They searched the faces of the crowd as they pushed their way through to the ticket booths in front of the wide tourist gangplank, but there was no sign of the nasty youth or the devious English pair. At the ticket booths, an attendant blocked their way.

"Sorry, ship's closed for the day, boys."

"But we have to get on right away!" Billy cried.

"No way, son," the attendant said, turning away. "Try next weekend."

Frustrated, they watched the attendant walk away across the wharf to where a final knot of tourists was coming down the gangplank.

"Next weekend!" Bob said in dismay. "Why isn't the ship open every day?"

"There probably isn't enough business until summer," guessed Jupe.

Suddenly Pete exclaimed, "Look! Up on the ship!"

High up on a top deck a gawky figure stood in the

twilight shadows. They saw a flash of teeth, and then the distant figure thumbed its nose directly at them!

"Skinny," Pete groaned.

Jupiter searched furiously with his eyes. A wide freight gate at the right edge of the wharf was still open. Jupiter glanced quickly at the ship attendants, who were ushering some tourists out through the last open ticket gate. No one was looking at the boys.

"Hurry, men," the stocky leader said.

They slipped through the unlocked freight gate and ran for the wide gangplank. Pete, in the lead, reached the gangway first—and ran full tilt into a tall man coming off the ship!

"Oooofff!" the Second Investigator grunted.

The man, who wore the uniform of a ship's captain, caught Pete to save him from falling.

"Easy, son," he said in a deep voice. "I'm sorry, but the ship is closed for the day."

"We know, sir," Jupiter said, "but we—"

"You know? Then I suggest you leave the wharf."

Behind them, some of the gate attendants looked at the boys angrily and motioned them out.

"Captain," Jupiter said desperately, "can we talk to you?"

The tall man smiled. "I'm not an actual captain, boys, just the exhibition manager. But call me Captain if you like. I'm happy to talk to any visitors to the ship, but right now I'm afraid—"

"We're not visitors, we're detectives," Billy blurted out. "We're on a case! Show him our card, Jupiter."

Jupiter handed the Captain the Investigators' card. "Amateur detectives, sir, but we are on a real case, and we know that something is hidden on your ship."

The Captain read the card and looked up. "Something hidden on the ship?"

"A fortune in gems, sir!" Pete exclaimed.

"A fortune? Hmmmmm, perhaps that explains it."

A few gate attendants approached impatiently, but the Captain waved them away. He looked at the boys intently.

"A lot of beds in our cabins were moved around today," he said. "We thought it was some prank. You're sure it isn't, boys?"

"No, sir," Jupiter said, "and you've just proven that someone else is looking for the gems! They're hidden in, or near, one of the ship's beds!" and he explained the crazy will and Dingo Towne's challenge. "We've solved all the riddles up to the last. Now all we have to do is find the right bed—if we're not too late."

"You may be," the Captain said. "A lot of beds were moved. But even if the gems haven't been found yet, how do you expect to find the right bed? We have five hundred!"

Jupiter swallowed, and the others groaned.

"F–five hundred beds?" Bob stammered.

"Two or three in a cabin, sometimes, but yes," the Captain said, "five hundred."

"Isn't their some special Queen's bed?" Pete asked.

"No, we don't have a royal suite on this ship."

"What about a queen-sized bed?" suggested Bob.

" 'Fraid not. This ship retired from service before extra-large beds became popular."

Jupiter slowly shook his head.

"There must be some direct way to find the exact

bed," he said. "Captain, did the *Queen* ever sail to Australia?"

"Many times. Years ago it was on a regular London-Australia-Canada run. You're thinking your Dingo sailed on her once?"

"The *old Ned* isn't usually just any bed, but a man's own bed," Jupiter said. "Are there old passenger lists, perhaps?"

"Yes—but in London! Your riddle wouldn't send you there."

Pete groaned. "With Dingo, I wouldn't be surprised!"

"There has to be a definite lead to the right bed," Jupiter insisted. "If we only had more time! With Skinny still on board, I don't think the gems have been found yet, but Skinny or someone else could find them at any moment!"

"Skinny?" the Captain snapped. "You mean there's someone still aboard ship? We'll just see about that!"

He strode toward the gangway with the boys following him. Jupiter lagged behind, lost in thought. Suddenly he raised his head.

"Fellows, I think there's only one possible—" His eyes widened. "The lifeboat! Look out!"

High above, one of the ship's lifeboats plunged down from its forward davit, swung in a wide, crashing arc against the ship's side, and sent oars, barrels, boxes, and other heavy equipment hurtling down toward the Captain and the boys!

"Jump!" the Captain cried as he pushed Pete and grabbed Billy.

Bob dove under the gangway, Pete staggered out of range, and Jupiter was too far away to be hit. The

Captain sprawled on top of Billy and just missed being hit by a barrel.

For a moment no one moved. Then, unhurt, they began to scramble up. Attendants were running toward them. The Captain looked up at the lifeboat dangling from its one davit and paled. He spoke quickly to the attendants:

"Go up and secure that boat." He looked at the boys. "Stay clear now—that might not have been an accident. Those ropes are checked very carefully."

"Skinny!" Bob fumed.

"I don't think so," Jupiter said. "We could have been killed, and even Skinny wouldn't do anything that dangerous."

"Then let's find out who it was!" Billy said, starting toward the gangway again.

"Stop!" the Captain commanded. "I'm sorry, boys, but I can't let you on the ship now. It could be too dangerous. I think this is a matter for the police."

"Yes, sir," Jupiter said quietly, "I think you're right. Call Chief Reynolds, and Bob will explain to him what's happened. Pete, stay here on the wharf with Billy until the police arrive."

Pete and Bob stared at their stocky leader.

"What are you going to do, Jupe?" Bob asked.

"I hope," Jupiter said, "that I'm going to find the *old Ned* without having to search the whole ship! Give me an hour, and if I'm not back tell the Chief to start searching the ship!"

While the others gaped, the stout boy ran back to his bike outside the gates and rode off into the dusk.

19 + Dead Man's Laugh!

An hour later, Bob, Pete, and Billy stood with the Captain and Chief Reynolds under the wharf flood-lights. Beside them, the great ship towered upward into the darkness. The Captain looked at his watch.

"Almost eight o'clock, Chief. The boy's had his hour," he said. "I don't think we should wait any longer. There's no telling what mischief is going on aboard our ship."

"If he locates the exact bed, it will save a lot of time," Chief Reynolds pointed out. "Jupiter is a resourceful boy. I'll give him fifteen more minutes."

"He'll be here!" Bob and Pete exclaimed in unison.

Chief Reynolds smiled. "I'm sure he will be, boys."

"Listen!" Billy cried. "That must be him now!"

Footsteps hurried along the wharf. Bob and Pete started forward to meet the First Investigator. They stopped. Roger Callow came walking rapidly through the gates and up to the group. He looked relieved.

"There you are, boys—and Billy's with you," the lawyer said. "Mrs. Towne said you had gone together to the town hall, but when I couldn't find you there I got nervous. So I called the police station. They told me Chief Reynolds was here with you."

"We're on the last clue, Mr. Callow," Bob said, and explained what the last riddle meant. "But we're afraid someone's on the ship, and maybe has the gems already!"

"Then what are we standing around for?" Callow demanded.

"Jupiter had an idea of how to get the exact room," Pete said. "We're waiting for him, only he's late."

"If we all split up," Mr. Callow said, "I'm sure we could locate—"

"That," a voice said, "would take a great deal of luck."

"Jupiter!" Billy cried.

The stout First Investigator walked through the gate. He looked at Mr. Callow.

"How did you get here, sir?" he asked.

"I was looking for you boys," the lawyer said, "but never mind that. Did you locate the right room, Jupiter?"

Jupiter nodded happily. "There was only one simple way to find out if Dingo had sailed on the *Queen*, and in what cabin: ask someone who might have sailed with him! Only two people were likely to have done that, I decided—Jack Dillon or the other friend who witnessed the will, Sadie Jingle."

"Did they?" Bob demanded.

"Mrs. Jingle did. She sailed from Australia with Dingo thirty years ago! I think Dingo named her a witness just to make her known to us! Anyway—" he grinned—"I've got the answer!"

"Then let's go aboard," the Captain said.

He led them up the gangplank onto the main deck—A-Deck. Few lights burned on the great ship. Dim passageways faded into the distance, and the shadowy topdecks above A could not be seen. Chief Reynolds stationed men at the gangway and other key points. The searchers all entered the vast, luxurious First-Class concourse. Jupiter picked up a tourist brochure from a pile on a table and started to study the deck plan printed in it.

"Which room is it, Jupiter?" Chief Reynolds asked.

"Here it is—Cabin 22, on D-Deck. Mrs. Jingle was next door in Cabin 21. She laughed when I asked her if she were sure—said she'd never forget the cabins because they were the worst on the ship! 'Right under the ruddy bows,' she said. She thought Dingo had the lower bunk, but I don't think the gems are *in* the bed." He tucked the deck plan in his pocket and pulled out his copy of the riddles. "The sixth and last riddle says:

> *In the posh Queen's old Ned, be bright*
> *and natural and the prize is yours.*

"When you talk about a bed, *be natural* must mean to lie down on it, and *be bright,* I'm convinced, is a double clue—meaning be clever and look for something *bright.*"

"Gosh, Jupiter," Billy said, "what would that be?"

"I think it should be a light we can see when we lie down on the bed!"

"Then let's go see!" the Captain said. "We'll have to walk all the way down—the elevators are shut off."

As they started down Pete cocked his head and listened.

"What was that? I heard a noise!"

They all listened. There was no sound anywhere.

"It sounded like someone bumping a wall," Pete said.

"Probably one of us, and we didn't notice," the Captain said. "D-Deck's the last down. It's dim, so step carefully."

They went down and down, the stairs narrowing with every deck. On D-Deck they turned forward toward Tourist Class. As they stepped through a watertight doorway into the area of smaller cabins, they all heard the sound ahead—a muffled, grunting sound!

"Now, that's a real noise!" Pete declared.

"Rats, I expect," Chief Reynolds said. "All ships have them."

"Not in our passenger cabins!" the Captain answered coldly. "Anyway, it's too loud for a rat."

Cautiously, they moved ahead along the dim passage. The strained grunting sound came from a narrow cabin. From a closet!

"Stand back, boys," Chief Reynolds said, and opened the closet door.

"Skinny!" the four boys cried at once.

The tall youth was stuffed into the closet like a bag of laundry, his hands and feet tied and his mouth gagged. He made a grunting sound as he strained to speak, and his eyes rolled wildly. Two of Chief Reynolds' men untied him and helped him out.

Strangely subdued, the nasty boy staggered to a bunk. "I've been in there for hours and hours! I . . . I'd just started searching the cabins down here when someone grabbed me from behind and hit me on the head."

"That's a lie!" Bob declared. "We saw you on deck only an hour or so ago!"

"It must have been someone pretending to be me," Skinny said, shivering. He sounded weak, scared, and beaten. "I was gagged and tied and shoved into that closet. I thought I'd never get out!"

"That'll teach you not to be so sneaky!" Pete said.

"Was it one person, or two?" Jupiter asked slowly.

Skinny shook his head. "I don't know. I never really saw the person—I was too woozy." Gingerly he felt the goose egg on his head.

Suddenly, from somewhere ahead in the ship, there was a crash like glass falling. The Captain came alert.

"That sounded like it was near Cabin 22!" he said.

"Hurry!" Jupiter cried.

Skinny didn't move. "Not me. You can have the gems."

Chief Reynolds left a man with Skinny, and the rest of them ran along the narrow passages behind the Captain. As they went around a final corner, the Captain pointed.

"That's D-22 up ahead!"

"Look!" Pete cried.

Winifred Percival came out of D-22 followed by the fat Cecil! They saw the group coming and ran the opposite way. Cecil was clutching a small, black case.

"Stop!" Chief Reynolds shouted. "Police!"

But the English pair only ran faster, the fat man shaking like jelly as he pounded behind his skinny sister. They scrambled up several flights of stairs, closely pursued, and darted through a door into the Tourist Lounge on B-Deck.

"The exit's on the left," the Captain panted. "We'll cut them off!"

He and Pete raced along the corridor and around to the other door, while the rest blocked the main doorway. Winifred saw Pete and the Captain appear at the exit. She changed direction quickly, running suddenly toward the entrance to the adjoining writing room. Fat Cecil tried to follow her sharp turn, failed, skidded, and flailed off balance. The black case flew away as he crashed against three tables and the wall, and ended up panting on the floor in a grotesque heap.

Winifred, seeing the disaster, stopped. She glared back at her fallen brother. "You fat idiot!"

The fat man was still trying to untangle himself when the Captain and Chief Reynolds hauled him to his feet. One of the Chief's men held Winifred. Jupiter picked up the black case.

"They must have overheard what I said up above," Jupiter guessed. "That was the noise Pete heard. They were running down ahead of us. Where did you find the case, Miss Percival? In a light fixture in Cabin D-22?"

Winifred nodded bleakly. "In the ceiling beyond the fixture."

"Open the case, Jupe," Bob urged.

Jupiter opened the case and they all stared at the glittering stones. Then Chief Reynolds bent forward. He picked up one of the sparkling green stones and studied it.

"This isn't an emerald, it's a piece of glass!" He rummaged among the stones. "They're all just glass. Fakes!"

Bob pointed. "There's an envelope under them."

The Chief drew out the envelope. Inside was a letter on a piece of light cardboard. He read it aloud:

> *To All Eager Fortune Hunters:*
> *You should have known a sane man would use his money wisely—I spent it! But it amused me to imagine a greedy horde pounding around on the trail of my loot. So here it is—a prize for fools!*
>
> *Dingo*

They stood stunned. Billy gasped:

"You mean, it was all . . . a trick?"

Jupiter's voice was weak. "I was so sure—"

"A lousy game!" Pete cried.

Roger Callow cried, "There must be more!" He whirled on the Percivals. "What else did you find in that ceiling?"

"Nothing," Cecil raged. "If you think the real gems were there, too, go look yourself!"

Jupiter said, "What else could he have hidden, Mr. Callow?"

"There must be something," Callow said. "Let's go look!"

Everyone trooped back downstairs to the cabin, with Chief Reynolds' men bringing Cecil and Winifred. The light fixture hung by a hinge from the ceiling, revealing a dark space beyond. Pete reached up into the hole, carefully avoiding the electrical wires. He felt around, began to shake his head, and then stopped. He drew out an envelope.

Roger Callow grabbed it and opened it. "It's the real will! The one that leaves everything to Nelly and Billy!" He laughed.

"But—that's not possible!" cried Jupiter.

"Why not?" said Roger Callow sharply.

"I mean," Jupiter said slowly, "if that's the will that was missing from your law office, why would it be hidden here?"

"Dingo wanted to make sure no one tried to destroy it, of course," Roger Callow said. "He knew the Percivals would try to get their hands on his money!" He looked triumphantly at the defeated English couple.

"But," Jupiter objected, "if that will was never found, Billy would still get all the money. And there isn't any money left anyway, Dingo says, so why hide this will?"

"You never know what a crazy man will do," Roger Callow said with a shrug. "At least this will gives Billy and Nelly a clear claim to the houses and the land."

"Yes," Jupiter said thoughtfully. "Well, I guess it was all a trick."

Billy cried, "I don't believe it! That letter the Chief has is a fake!"

"It could be," Bob said. "Maybe—"

Pete said, "Chief, what's that hanging from the letter?"

"It's a piece of string," Bob said.

The Chief examined the short piece of string that was attached to the back of the letter they'd found under the fake gemstones. He pulled it slowly.

A laugh echoed through the cabin!

"It's a string recording," Jupiter exclaimed.

"It's Granddad's laugh!" Billy cried.

The dead man's laugh filled the cabin.

20 ⊹ Jupiter Sets a Trap

"A practical joke, and nothing more!" Chief Reynolds said in disgust. "You're sure that's your grandfather's laugh, young Towne?"

Billy nodded miserably. "It's Granddad all right. He . . . he must have made that string recording of his own laugh!"

"And he must have been crazy to play such a grisly joke on the people he left behind," the Chief said.

"All a joke!" Winifred Percival wailed. "The old villain!"

Chief Reynolds turned to the woman sternly. "For you and your brother it's more than a joke, madam. Captain, did these two have permission to be on this ship after it closed? Or to break into ship's property?"

"Certainly not!" the Captain snapped.

"Which makes them guilty of breaking and entering," the Chief said.

Cecil sputtered, "You can't accuse us—!"

"Not to mention dropping that lifeboat on us," Jupiter said.

The Chief said seriously, "That's a very strong charge."

"Idiot!" Winifred suddenly cried at Cecil. "I told you not to do that! Now look at the mess we're in!"

"Be quiet!" Cecil raged. "The stupid boy—"

But Winifred turned to Chief Reynolds. "It was his idea! The lifeboat, the theft, everything! All his insane plan!"

Jupiter grinned. "I thought they did it to scare us off the ship and gain time—but I wasn't sure. They tried a similar trick this morning, when they locked Billy in a van."

"What!" screeched Winifred. "We never—"

"Take them away," Chief Reynolds told his men abruptly.

Two patrolmen took hold of the Percivals. Cecil tried to slug Winifred, but the patrolman held him back.

"They didn't know, you fool!" Cecil raged.

"You had to come here, you fat toad!" Winifred shouted.

"You were drooling for your share, you sour prune!"

The two patrolmen dragged them out, and they disappeared down the passageway still screaming at each other. Chief Reynolds shook his head, almost laughing.

"I'm not sure we wouldn't punish them more by making them go back to England with each other," he said.

He and the Captain went out, followed by Billy and Roger Callow. The lawyer carried the envelope that contained the earlier will. Bob and Pete started to leave, too, but Jupiter said to them:

"Let them go ahead, fellows."

At the door, Roger Callow looked back questioningly.

"We'll be right with you," Jupiter said to him. The

lawyer shrugged and left.

Pete and Bob looked at Jupiter in surprise.

"But, Jupe," Bob said, "it's all over."

"A rotten joke," Pete said.

Jupiter was studying the deck plan again. He gave a grunt of satisfaction and looked up. "No, I don't think it was just a joke, and I don't think it's over. I think this is Dingo's last, and best, trick!"

"But there aren't any more riddles," Pete exclaimed. "We solved the last one, and got the prize—fake gemstones!"

"No," Jupiter said again, "I don't think we've solved the last riddle. I'm convinced there's a cleverly concealed *seventh* riddle!"

He took out his copy of the riddles. "Look, after what seems to be the last riddle—the sixth—there are two more sentences: *Who'd have thought the old man had so much money in him? Roll the dice and the swag is yours!*"

"Just rubbing his challenge in, Jupe," Bob said. "Dingo liked to laugh at people, taunt them."

"That's what I thought, too," Jupiter agreed. "But now . . . Take that first extra sentence: *Who'd have thought the old man had so much money in him?* It's almost an exact quote from Shakespeare's play *Macbeth*—'Who would have thought the old man to have had so much blood in him?' That's no coincidence."

"Maybe he just liked *Macbeth*," Pete said. "Anyway, why does that make you think there's a seventh riddle?"

"Because the quote doesn't have any reason to be in the will otherwise," Jupiter said. "And because I'm sure that old miser wouldn't have spent all his money, and because he used gambling talk."

"Gambling?" Bob said. "What's that got to do with an extra riddle, Jupe?"

"He says, *Roll the dice and the swag is yours*," Jupiter read from the page of riddles. "Why say *roll the dice* when he could have said a lot of other things there?"

"Who knows?" Pete groaned.

"I think I do," Jupiter stated. "Fellows, what does the word *natural* mean in a dice game?"

Bob's eyes widened. "A *natural* is a seven or eleven on the first throw—I read it in a games book! A *seven!* Dingo *was* telling us there's a hidden seventh riddle!"

"Wow!" Pete cried. "But what is the seventh riddle? Something in that quote that's almost like *Macbeth*?"

"It has to be," Jupiter said—and suddenly stopped talking. He seemed to listen for a moment. Then he went on in a much louder voice. "But I can't figure out what it means. I admit I'm stumped. Maybe we'd better tell the others and see what they can think of."

"Gee, why not try to find it ourselves, Jupe?" Pete asked. "The Percivals and Skinny are all out of the way now."

"No," Jupiter said loudly, "we need help now. Come on."

The stout First Investigator led them out of the cabin and back to the main stairway. They went on up to the First Class concourse and stepped out onto the dark, silent deck of the great ship. Jupiter stopped and quickly pulled the other two into the shadows.

"This is far enough, fellows," the stocky leader of the trio whispered.

Pete said, "Far enough? For what, Jupe?"

"What are we doing?" Bob whispered, mystified.

"We're waiting a few more minutes," Jupiter said, "and then we're going down to where the gems are!"

"You know where they are?" Bob exclaimed softly.

"Where?" Pete said almost loudly.

Jupiter glanced quickly around, but nothing moved on the dark deck. "On the deck plan of the *Queen* there's a small lounge called the Macbeth Room! That's where they are!"

"Gosh, then why did you say you were stumped?" Pete asked.

"You'll soon see," Jupiter said maddeningly. He looked at his watch. "All right, let's go. Be very quiet. Just stay behind me and do what I do."

The First Investigator stepped as quietly as a cat back into the main concourse and down the wide, carpeted stairs to B-Deck. Bob and Pete silently followed. He led them through dim passageways on B-Deck, and stopped in the shadows by a door with a circular window in it.

"It's the side service door to the Macbeth Room," he whispered.

"What do we do now?" Pete whispered back.

"We wait," Jupiter answered low, "and we watch."

Even as he said it, a beam of light suddenly stabbed through the room. Without moving forward, it quickly probed all around the plush lounge, illuminating a series of tables and low armchairs upholstered in plaid, a rustic bar, walls decorated with ancient helmets and shields, and pedestals with busts of fiercely bearded Scottish warriors.

The person with the flashlight began to move around the room.

Holding their breath, the three boys watched the light dart among the tables of the dark cocktail lounge. Except for the hand holding the flashlight, they could see nothing of the person—only a black shape that moved quickly about, pausing at each table, searching under the bar, probing the shields and helmets that hung on the walls. From time to time the person's free hand appeared in the light, reaching out to rip objects from walls and tables, holding them close for examination, then hurling them away.

Then the beam of light swept across the busts of the warriors, swept back over them again—and came to rest on the bronze head of one with a thick beard and a royal crown. With a sharp grunt, the shadowy figure moved to the kingly bust and picked it up. There was an exclamation of triumph as the hand of the searcher seemed to test the weight of the bronze bust.

Jupiter's hand squeezed Bob's shoulder, almost making the smaller boy cry out. Jupiter whispered, "He's found out it's hollow! He's got it!"

The three boys watched the dark shadow lay the flashlight on a table and reach its hand up into the hollow bronze bust. A large, leather bag came out of the bust! Dropping the bust with a crash, the hands opened the bag. The grunt was one of triumph this time. The shadowy shape turned to the main door of the Macbeth Room and vanished through it.

"Hurry," Jupiter whispered. "Follow him, but don't make any noise!"

They peered around the corner of the main B-Deck passageway and saw the figure hurrying away in the dim light. A quick glimpse, and the person disappeared into another side passageway. The boys reached the side passage just in time to see him go into a cabin. They crept up to the cabin entrance.

Inside, the dark figure worked inside a small closet. Then he backed out, no longer holding the leather bag! Jupiter tapped both Bob and Pete and pointed urgently to another cabin across the passage.

Silently the boys slipped into the second cabin. They had barely crouched down when the figure came out of the first cabin and hurried away toward the main passage again. Pete moved to follow. Jupiter stopped him.

"No, Pete, let him go. Let's find that bag."

He went across to the first cabin and opened the closet door. Bob and Pete watched the stocky boy take out his pencil flashlight and shine it into the closet. There was a ventilation grating in the closet wall, and the leather bag was faintly visible behind it. Jupiter's eyes glowed—but he closed the closet door again!

"They must be the gems!" Pete cried softly. "Aren't we going to take them, Jupe? Or even look at them?"

"And go after that thief?" Bob added. "I mean, whoever that was had to be stealing the jewels, right?"

"There's no doubt of it," Jupiter said, "but he won't go far, and we mustn't touch the bag. It's the proof that will expose the thief!"

"You set a trap, didn't you?" Bob realized. "You knew someone would steal the gems from the Macbeth

Room! How, Jupe?"

"Because I happened to know that the will we found with the glass gems was a fake! Dingo never put it there. That meant someone had already found the fake gems—and put them back!"

"Put them back?" Pete said, puzzled.

"So *we* wouldn't be suspicious, and would still lead the thief to the real gems! That's when I realized we'd been followed all along by whoever owed money to Savo and Turk, and was sure the person would still be watching us. So I set the trap.

"I solved the hidden seventh riddle out loud, and then pretended to be stumped. I knew the Macbeth Room was a ship's lounge, and I was pretty sure the thief knew that, too, and would go after the gems if he thought we were off the ship!"

"And he did!" Pete exclaimed.

"Yes," Jupiter said happily. "Now we'll find Chief Reynolds and show him how the gems were rehidden so the thief could come back and get them later. The bag plus the fingerprints on the grating will be enough proof. So—"

"So I'll have to eliminate you boys after all."

They whirled. Roger Callow stood in the open doorway of the cabin with a pistol in his hand.

21 ✦ Pete Saves the Day

"Too bad," the lawyer said grimly. "I thought I could let you go after I got the gems."

"You planned to steal them all along!" Bob exclaimed hotly.

Callow stepped closer, his pistol steady, and he smiled angrily.

"I had to have the money, and that old bandit tried to block me with that crazy will," he said furiously. "He didn't want me to marry Nelly—he guessed I was after his money. But now I'll get it all!"

"You were using us," Jupiter said slowly. "That's why you hired us instead of an adult agency. You thought kids would be easier to fool."

"Apparently I was wrong," Callow said. "You three are just too smart for your own good."

He waved the pistol menacingly. The boys turned pale but stood their ground.

"I can see why you wanted the gems found before anyone else could steal them," Bob said, "but why steal them yourself? They'd be partly yours anyway after you married Mrs. Towne."

"You made sure of that, didn't you?" added Jupe. "By planting a fake copy of the earlier will that named Nelly Towne."

"Smart boy!" Callow said. "But I need more than just

part of the jewels—and I wouldn't care to explain why to Nelly."

"We know why!" Pete blurted out.

"Because you lost a lot of money gambling with Mr. Savo and Turk!" Bob added fiercely.

"And Nelly would be very unhappy to learn you have enormous gambling debts," concluded Jupiter.

"So? You know a lot too much, don't you? That's very unfortunate," Roger Callow said. "But you're right. Nelly would probably break up with me if she knew why I needed so much of her money. Anyway, why share the gems with her and Billy when they can all be mine? No one will ever find them now, and I'll marry Nelly and get the houses and land, too!"

The lawyer laughed, keeping the ugly pistol pointed at the boys. Jupiter stared past Callow at the open doorway of the cabin.

"No, you won't," the stout boy said. "Mrs. Towne will never marry you when she finds out you've stolen her fortune."

Callow's smile was evil, "But she isn't going to find out, is she? Only you three know that I found the gems, and you won't tell anyone, I'm afraid."

"Perhaps we won't," Jupiter said bravely, "but she'll find out anyway—won't she, Billy? Hurry, go and tell the Chief what you've heard!"

Callow looked straight at Jupiter and laughed again. He shook his head.

"An old trick, Jupiter. I'm afraid it won't work," he said.

"Quickly, Billy!" Pete urged.

Callow scowled. "Stop it! The three of you aren't strong enough to overpower me anyway, even if your childish trick made me turn around."

"Go on, Billy!" Jupiter said almost in panic. "Run!"

Roger Callow's eyes narrowed at the panic in Jupiter's voice. Then he heard the noise behind him, and turned at last—but too late! Billy, who had been standing in the dim passageway staring at the boys and Callow, was already running away!

"He's made it!" Pete cried happily.

Roger Callow swore as he stared after the fast-disappearing little boy. Then he turned slowly back to The Three Investigators.

"Greed ruined you, Mr. Callow," Jupiter said. "Now you'll lose everything, no matter what you do to us!"

The lawyer nodded. "Yes, that was cleverly done, I admit it. You really fooled me by talking straight to Billy. I was sure it was only a trick. My congratulations."

"And we're no danger to you anymore," Jupiter pointed out.

"No, you're not," Callow said, "but you're going to be a help to me. Fortunately, I had an alternate plan for just such an emergency. Pete, you will step into that closet and retrieve that bag of jewels!" The lawyer leveled his pistol firmly. "Don't try any brave tricks. The noise of a pistol shot makes no difference to me now!"

Pete gulped and did as he was told. After unscrewing the ventilation grating, he handed out the bag of jewels. The lawyer took the bag and sighed.

"Since the jig is now up, as they say, a small trip with the gems is indicated," he said. "Once I'm gone, I doubt that anyone could identify these gems. I think Mexico is quite pleasant this time of year, especially for a rich man." He waved the pistol. "Now walk ahead of me. Left at the door."

The boys moved along the dim passageways, prodded and directed by Roger Callow's pistol. They all heard the noise of Chief Reynolds and his men hurrying down to the cabin they had just left. Roger Callow listened carefully, then urged the boys down some stairs and through a maze of passageways in the bowels of the great ship. Distant, urgent shouts were heard as the police found Callow and the boys gone from the cabin.

Roger Callow looked down a cross passageway on C-Deck. He motioned to Bob and Jupiter.

"You two walk that way! Now!"

"But—" Bob began to protest.

"Pete comes with me," Callow snapped. "If you want to see your friend again, walk down that corridor and don't look back!"

Bob and Jupiter did what they were told. They reached the far end of the passageway before they dared to turn around and run back.

Roger Callow and Pete were gone!

The two boys began to shout and yell, and tried to find their way through the passages to the Chief and his men. At last they were heard, and after many shouts back and forth, everyone met in an open concourse on B-Deck.

"Where is Callow?" Chief Reynolds demanded.

Bob and Jupiter quickly told him what had happened.

"Callow's right. If he reaches Mexico we won't be able to prove he stole the gems," the Chief said. "But he won't get away. My men are covering the gangplank."

Jupiter frowned. "Is that the only way off the ship, Chief? Callow said he had a plan of escape—and he seemed to be heading down."

"The gangplank is the only way to the wharf that I know of," the Chief said.

The Captain seemed to snap alert.

"The wharf, Chief?" he said. "What about our freight port back near the stern? Is that guarded?"

"No!" the Chief said. "I didn't know it was open!"

"It's not supposed to be, but—" the Captain said.

"Hurry, Chief!" Jupiter cried.

The Captain took them through the silent heart of the giant ship down to the freight receiving area. The doors to it had been forced open. Inside, he pointed ahead to the high freight port.

"It's open!"

They rushed forward to the open port. Roger Callow was on the steep, narrow freight gangplank that led down to the dark wharf, well away from the guarded tourists' gangway. He held Pete in front of him, his pistol pointing at the tall boy's head, and backed slowly down the swaying plank.

"Stay back," Callow shouted, "and stay where you are!"

"Callow!" Chief Reynolds cried. "You can't get away!"

"Yes I can! Unless you want this kid shot!"

He got no farther. Distracted for a moment by the people on the ship, he never saw Pete quickly thrust his foot back. The boy hooked the lawyer's ankle and pushed backward. Callow lost his balance and fell against the narrow gangplank rail, pulling Pete back with him. Flailing wildly, he went over the rail backward with Pete, losing his pistol and the bag of gems!

They plummeted down toward the water thirty feet below—Callow, Pete, the pistol, and the gems! With a cry of rage, Roger Callow struck the water with his leg twisted under him, and came up sputtering and screaming that his leg was broken!

Pete, the athlete of the Investigators, made a powerful flipover, grabbed the bag of gems in mid-air, and went into a spectacular dive that cut the surface cleanly! He came up with a wide grin and the bag of gems held high.

As the Captain and Billy applauded, Pete swam to a ladder on the side of the wharf. Chief Reynolds' men fished out Roger Callow. Holding his leg, and looking like a drowned rat, the lawyer slumped on the wharf between two policemen.

"He'll do no more thieving," the Chief said sternly, and turned to Jupiter just as sternly. "But you shouldn't have tried to catch him by yourself, Jupiter. You should have told me what you suspected."

"There was no proof, sir," Jupiter said. "He hadn't done anything yet except plant a fake will—and I couldn't prove that. If we hadn't trapped him, he could have married Mrs. Towne and got her fortune."

"Well," the Chief said, "perhaps in that case . . ."

"You see," Jupiter went on, "I was sure his greed would defeat him if we gave him what looked like a safe chance to steal the gems all for himself."

"The gems!" Billy cried.

They all turned to Pete. The Second Investigator had opened the bag and poured the contents out onto the deck. A mound of red, yellow, blue, and green gemstones shimmered in the dim light from the giant ship. Everyone grinned at the magnificent display!

22 ✦ Jupiter Confesses an Error!

Several days later, the Three Investigators sat in Hector Sebastian's living room and reported on the case of the dead man's riddle. Their mentor leaned back in his chair as he listened intently to the boys.

"Son of a gun," he finally said. "So Roger Callow was really after Dingo's money from the start."

"So it seems," Jupiter said.

"What a lowlife!"

"Old Dingo suspected him of being a fortune hunter," Pete said, "but Mrs. Towne wouldn't listen to Dingo."

"Love is often blind," the mystery writer mused. "Did Dingo cook up that crazy will to outwit Callow?"

"Partly," said Jupiter. "He thought the treasure hunt would slow Callow down and perhaps make him expose his real motives in courting Nelly. He told Jack Dillon he'd show the lawyer some real fortune-hunting! But mostly Dingo was disgusted with Mrs. Towne for falling for Callow—at least, that's what Mr. Dillon says. Dingo really hoped somebody else would find the treasure and keep it—because his relatives didn't deserve it!"

"Mr. Callow sure was double-stunned!" added Pete. "First he found that the earlier will was missing from his office, then the crazy will was filed!"

"You mean Callow didn't destroy the earlier will himself?" asked Mr. Sebastian.

"No, Dingo did! He stole it from Callow's office," answered Jupiter.

"But Mr. Callow would have destroyed the crazy will fast enough!" put in Bob. "And that's just why Dingo left it with Jack Dillon."

Jupe went on: "Callow had to act fast when the crazy will was filed. He was desperate for money to pay his gambling debts, he was afraid someone else would find the jewels first and steal them—and he was initially stumped by the riddles. So he hired us."

"As dupes," continued Bob, "to point the way to the jewels. He was sure he could get rid of us easily if we got in his way at the end."

"A bad move on his part," the mystery writer said, his eyes twinkling.

"Actually, he defeated himself," Jupiter said modestly. "When we did lead him to the gems, his greed ruined him."

"What made you suspect Roger Callow's motives?" asked Mr. Sebastian.

Jupiter took a deep breath. He always enjoyed an opportunity to show off his reasoning ability. "Well, I first became suspicious when Turk and Savo let slip the reason for our being locked up—that some gambler wanted to reach the jewels first. Now, Turk and Savo had watched the Towne house as much as they'd watched us. This made it likely that the gambler could be found there. Who was there a lot? Only Mrs. Towne and Roger Callow.

"Then, why wasn't Billy picked up, too? Obviously because the gambler didn't know that Billy was working with us. Mrs. Towne did because we told her. But Roger Callow probably didn't know yet. And neither did the Percivals—or whoever locked Billy in the van earlier.

"So, when we went down to the ship, I knew Callow was a possibility for the gambler—but only a possibility. Then something happened to make me sure he was the culprit. We found the fake will behind the ceiling fixture in the cabin."

"But how did you know it was a fake—and that Roger was guilty?" asked Mr. Sebastian.

"Because Sadie Jingle had told me that Dingo had destroyed the earlier will!" Jupe announced triumphantly. "When she and Jack Dillon were called on to witness the riddle will, Dingo mentioned he'd stolen back and burned the other one. He wanted them to speak up if a so-called earlier will ever showed up. He said he wouldn't put it past Callow to forge one—and he was right!

"Well, once that earlier will appeared, it was simple to figure out who had placed it with the fake jewels—and why!"

"Keep going," said Mr. Sebastian.

"Yeah, go through it all," said Pete. "I'm still not sure I follow this part of it."

"Okay," said Jupiter. "It's a simple matter of deciding who benefits. Now, before this fake will showed up, Billy was in line to get everything as the only direct descendant. Nobody could touch his money—not even his mother.

"Then the fake will comes to light, naming Billy and Nelly Towne. Billy benefits again, but only half as much as before. Mrs. Towne benefits now—she gets half the fortune. And if Roger Callow marries her, *he* benefits—because in California a husband automatically gets half of his wife's property."

"Yes, under the communal property laws," agreed Mr. Sebastian.

"Now, I didn't think Mrs. Towne would steal from her son. So that left Roger Callow as the only likely suspect. I surmised that he had been searching the ship all afternoon, after stuffing Billy in the van and telling Turk and Savo to pick us up. He found the fake jewels but couldn't guess where the real ones were—he wouldn't believe Dingo spent all his money any more than I did. Therefore, since he couldn't get to the treasure first, he planted the fake will to make sure he'd get something through Nelly. And he no doubt ordered Savo to release us so we could search and find the fake will and the real jewels. Of course, we had already escaped.

"As soon as I deduced this, I decided to set a trap and find out if Callow really was a thief. I hung back in that cabin, hoping he would eavesdrop—and he did! I solved the seventh riddle out loud and Callow ran right to the Macbeth Room—right into my trap!"

"A trap that almost caught you instead," Mr. Sebastian reminded him. "But it turned out all right in the end."

"Yes," Jupiter said, beaming.

"Jupe, you did some very quick thinking but you

made some lucky guesses, too," Mr. Sebastian said. "Admit it—accusing the Percivals of dropping that lifeboat was a shot in the dark."

"Actually, it wasn't," Jupiter answered. "Whoever dropped the boat wanted us kept off the ship, which meant they didn't know the gems in D-22 were fakes. Mr. Callow already knew, Skinny was tied up, and that left only the Percivals."

"You're right again," said the mystery writer. "Now what's going to happen to the wrongdoers in this case? Roger Callow is obviously headed for jail for his various crimes. What about the others?"

"Savo and Turk have disappeared," said Bob. "The police are hunting for them. The Percivals have been charged with reckless endangerment. They could be fined or jailed, but they may just be deported. Like Chief Reynolds said, the worst thing you could do to them is send them away together!"

"A great idea," said Mr. Sebastian. "And Skinny?"

"He swears his scare in the closet has reformed him."

"That sounds too good to be true," said Mr. Sebastian. "So once again, determined, methodical detective work pans out. I couldn't have done better myself. Congratulations."

"Thank you . . ." Jupiter began.

Suddenly, Bob and Pete began to roar with laughter. Mr. Sebastian looked at them in surprise. Jupiter went red-faced.

"What in the world—" Mr. Sebastian began.

"It's a joke on me," Jupiter broke in. "It seems we

could have skipped five riddles if I'd done a little more research."

"What do you mean?"

"Dingo used the word *posh* in front of *Queen*. I knew it meant elegant, first class, so I didn't research it," Jupiter said with a sigh. "Then the Captain of the *Queen* happened to tell us later what it meant. It seems *posh* was invented by Englishmen going to and from India. Because of the wind and sun, the best steamship cabins were on the left, or port, side going out to India, and on the right, or starboard, side coming home to England. So if you wanted to have the best, travel in the most comfort, you went Port Out, Starboard Home—P.O.S.H.: *posh*."

"Since the *Queen of the South* used to stop at India on the London–Australia run," Bob said, "Dingo was really giving us a shortcut clue—the *posh Queen!*"

"The only possible posh Queen around," Jupiter moaned, "and I missed it."

"Well, cheer up, so did everyone else," the mystery writer said. "Even without the shortcut you met a difficult challenge with brains and persistence. You all have a lot to be proud of."

As the Investigators filed out, Mr. Sebastian grinned to himself. He felt sorry for the next con man who made the mistake of underestimating Jupiter Jones and his friends.

THE THREE INVESTIGATORS MYSTERY SERIES

NOVELS

The Secret of Terror Castle
The Mystery of the Stuttering Parrot
The Mystery of the Whispering Mummy
The Mystery of the Green Ghost
The Mystery of the Vanishing Treasure
The Secret of Skeleton Island
The Mystery of the Fiery Eye
The Mystery of the Silver Spider
The Mystery of the Screaming Clock
The Mystery of the Moaning Cave
The Mystery of the Talking Skull
The Mystery of the Laughing Shadow
The Secret of the Crooked Cat
The Mystery of the Coughing Dragon
The Mystery of the Flaming Footprints
The Mystery of the Nervous Lion
The Mystery of the Singing Serpent
The Mystery of the Shrinking House
The Secret of Phantom Lake
The Mystery of Monster Mountain
The Secret of the Haunted Mirror
The Mystery of the Dead Man's Riddle
The Mystery of the Invisible Dog
The Mystery of Death Trap Mine
The Mystery of the Dancing Devil
The Mystery of the Headless Horse
The Mystery of the Magic Circle
The Mystery of the Deadly Double
The Mystery of the Sinister Scarecrow
The Secret of Shark Reef
The Mystery of the Scar-Faced Beggar
The Mystery of the Blazing Cliffs

(*Continued on next page*)

The Mystery of the Purple Pirate
The Mystery of the Wandering Cave Man
The Mystery of the Kidnapped Whale
The Mystery of the Missing Mermaid
The Mystery of the Two-Toed Pigeon
The Mystery of the Smashing Glass
The Mystery of the Trail of Terror
The Mystery of the Rogues' Reunion
The Mystery of the Creep-Show Crooks
The Mystery of Wreckers' Rock

FIND YOUR FATE™ MYSTERIES

The Case of the Weeping Coffin
The Case of the Dancing Dinosaur
The Case of the House of Horrors

PUZZLE BOOKS

The Three Investigators' Book of Mystery Puzzles